T0328874

Everyone has a secret. . . .

Suzanne—Now that she knows who her father is, will she risk everything to spend some time with him?

Nikki—Sure Suzanne saved her life, but now Nikki's wondering just how much she owes her new friend. . . .

Keith—If John won't help him pay off his debts, Keith may have to tell Katia that John's been cheating on her with Victoria.

Katia—She's been in a coma since the night of the car accident. Will she ever recover?

Sworn to Silence

Jennifer Baker

AN ARCHWAY PAPERBACK
Published by POCKET BOOKS
New York   London   Toronto   Sydney   Tokyo   Singapore

This book is a work of fiction. Names, characters, places, and incidents are either products of the author's imagination or are used fictitiously. Any resemblance to actual events or locales or persons, living or dead, is entirely coincidental.

AN ARCHWAY PAPERBACK *Original*

An Archway Paperback published by
POCKET BOOKS, a division of Simon & Schuster Inc.
1230 Avenue of the Americas, New York, NY 10020

Produced by Daniel Weiss Associates, Inc., New York

ISBN: 978-1-4814-2877-4

First Archway Paperback printing December 1995

10 9 8 7 6 5 4 3 2 1

AN ARCHWAY PAPERBACK and colophon are registered trademarks of Simon & Schuster Inc.

Printed in the U.S.A.

IL 7+

One

"Please don't let her die," Victoria Hill whimpered, pushing her damp red hair away from her swollen, tear-covered face.

She was huddled on the side of the road, feeling frantic and helpless. A few feet away three EMT workers were wrenching the passenger-side door off her vintage BMW. Katia Stein was stuck inside.

Victoria had been driving Katia home from Nikki Stewart's party when an oncoming car veered into their lane. She'd swerved to avoid a head-on collision, but her reaction had totaled the car.

The crash had happened in an instant, but to Victoria it seemed as if the sound of crumpling metal and shattering glass and screams—Katia's screams, her screams—had gone on for hours. She'd had plenty of time to realize she was dying.

1

But she hadn't died.

She'd awakened to new terrors.

When she came to, Victoria had discovered Katia slumped forward, the passenger-side door crumpled against her. Blood was trickling out of her mouth. She'd seemed entirely lifeless.

Katia. Her friend. Keith's sister. John Badillo's girlfriend.

The EMT workers removed the door, and Katia's motionless form was exposed to the rainy night. Victoria closed her eyes to block out the frightening scene, but in her mind's eye she saw something just as horrifying: the car that had run them off the road driving away moments after the crash. Leaving her alone, even though she was screaming for help, even though her friend might be dying!

The car had been a familiar red Jaguar. Her father's.

Why does it have to be like this? Victoria thought hopelessly. Her own father was responsible for this nightmare—and he'd been too much of a coward to stick around and admit what he had done. He'd obviously been too drunk even to recognize his own daughter's car—and then had sped away. . . .

After her father had deserted her, Victoria had waited—again for what seemed like hours—before a white Honda had come slowly down the road through the rain. Seeing the wreck, the car had pulled over immediately. A stout woman

2

wearing a beret and oversized glasses had emerged and taken over. She'd called 911 on her cellular phone and hadn't left Victoria's side until the emergency workers arrived. Then she'd mumbled something about being late and drove off. Victoria didn't even know her name.

Now, as Victoria watched, the EMT workers stepped away from the car and began to talk earnestly. Victoria had promised them she'd stay back, but she couldn't stop herself from rushing forward. "Don't just stand there—get her out!"

One of the EMT workers came and put an arm around Victoria. "We're doing everything we can. The best thing you can do for your friend is to stay calm."

"But what if she dies?" Victoria asked hysterically. *What if she dies and I'm the only one who knows who did it?*

Suzanne Willis's throat was raw from gulping in the cold night air. The clothes she had worn to Nikki's party were drenched, and rain dripped from her brown hair.

She had run the entire mile from Nikki's house, and she was gasping for air when she reached her front porch. Without stopping to catch her breath, she yanked her keys out of her purse, unlocked the door, and angrily thrust it open.

"Mom! Mom, I've got to talk to you *now!*"

No answer.

Jennifer Baker

The house was dark and quiet. Her mother wasn't home from her date with Mr. Houghton yet. Suzanne slammed the door with all of her strength and stormed into the kitchen. How *dare* her mother be out at a time like this?

Suzanne grabbed the phone book and looked up the number for the restaurant where her mother was supposed to be eating. She punched the numbers into the phone.

"Atlanta Grill," a voice chirped. "How may I help you this evening?"

Suzanne changed her mind and slammed the phone down. What she had to say to her mother could only be said in person. Her mother had to come home eventually. When she did, Suzanne would be there to confront her. All of her mother's hurtful lies echoed in her mind: "Your father doesn't know about you. I don't even know where he lives now." That night at Nikki's, Suzanne had discovered the truth. Her father lived right there in Hillcrest—and he was well aware of who she was.

Her own parents had conspired against her, but their deceitful little game was over now. Suzanne planned to tell the whole world—starting with her mother—what she had discovered.

"Good night, kid!" Mr. DeJesus said with a broad grin.

"Hurry home," Mr. Hammersmith called out. "We wouldn't want you to miss your curfew."

4

The men laughed and joked as Keith Stein shrugged his strong shoulders into his jacket and pulled a baseball cap on over his brown curls. He didn't understand why the older men were enjoying themselves so much. Both of them had lost money—and plenty of it—that night. Only one possible explanation for their happiness occurred to him: They were celebrating because Keith hadn't won. Those two geezers probably hated being beaten by someone young enough to be their son.

Mr. Martin pushed back his chair and got up to see Keith out. When they had crossed the small room, he put a hand on Keith's arm. "Don't take it too hard. Everyone has an off night now and again."

An off night? That was putting it mildly. The entire evening had been a total wash.

Keith had been miserable at Nikki's bash. It was the usual scene: Keith alone, surrounded by happy couples. Sometimes he felt as if he were the only guy at Hillcrest High without a girlfriend. Certainly he was the only guy on the football team without a girlfriend. Not a happy realization.

Rather than sit around and watch other people have a good time, he'd slipped out of the party and headed over to Mr. Martin's. Martin held a regular poker game in his basement. For the past few weeks, Keith had dominated the game. Every time he graced the old guys with his presence, he'd wiped them out.

Until that night.

Keith had arrived to discover that a new player had joined the game: Tony. He had won hand after hand.

As he reached the door, Keith nodded toward the dark-haired stranger still sitting at the card table. "Who is he, anyway?" Keith asked. "I've never seen him around Hillcrest before."

"Tony?" Mr. Martin looked uncomfortable. He glanced back at the others. They were within earshot, but for the moment the other men weren't paying attention to them. They were busy exchanging wisecracks.

Mr. Martin leaned toward Keith and lowered his voice. "Tony's a bookie." He seemed about to say more, but the other players started to get impatient.

"If we're going to play, let's play," Mr. Hammersmith called to Mr. Martin.

Tony looked up from the deck of cards he was shuffling and smirked at Keith. "Thanks for stopping by, kid. See you around."

"You can count on that," Keith said.

Tony slowly laid the deck on the table. "Do you mind if I give you some advice?"

Keith shrugged. He didn't care what this idiot had to say, but his mother had taught him to be polite.

"Stay in the small-stakes games," Tony said, sitting back in his chair and crossing his arms. "You're not ready to run with the big boys yet."

"I always won before tonight," Keith shot back.

"Beginner's luck," Tony said. "Trust me— more nights like this are ahead of you."

Keith couldn't get out of there fast enough. He didn't enjoy losing, but having this creep rub it in was too much.

When Keith got outside, the rain had let up, but moisture still hung in the air. The trees were dripping. He got into his shiny black Corvette, turned the ignition key, cranked up the radio, and pulled out onto the Martins' quiet street. The road was still wet. At the end of the block, he turned left toward home.

"Luck! Dumb luck!" Keith said, banging the palm of his hand against the steering wheel. It was unbelievable, but that night he'd lost most of the money he'd made over the past few weeks. Only a few hundred bucks were left in his wallet.

That hurt. No denying it. But Keith knew he'd lost the money because of a run of bad luck. Tony could say what he liked; Keith knew it had nothing to do with lack of skill. He'd gotten bad cards, that's all.

"What now?" Keith groaned when he spotted a pair of flares set out on the road ahead, forcing him to slow down. Just what he needed. More aggravation.

But Keith's irritation faded when he realized it was a real accident—looked pretty bad, too. A couple of ambulances stood on the side of the road, their spinning lights throwing garish flashes of red on the wet pavement.

Keith was moving onto the shoulder of the road to pass the accident scene when he recognized Victoria's BMW crumpled at the side of the road. The vintage car was the only one in Hillcrest. It had to be hers.

"Oh, no," Keith whispered as the awful realization sank in. Victoria had been in an accident. She might even be dead.

Keith and Victoria had dated briefly the year before. No big romance. After a few weeks she had moved on to other conquests. Although Keith hadn't been in love with Victoria, it had taken him several weeks to get over being dumped. After that, they had resumed a slightly uneasy friendship. Keith hadn't had much choice on that score—all of his friends were friends with Victoria. If he didn't want to be a social outcast, he had to get along with her.

Feeling a bit shaken, Keith pulled off the road and parked. He got out of the car and walked toward the accident.

"Victoria!" Keith started to run. He had caught sight of her, huddled under a blanket by the side of the road. She looked lost. "Victoria, are you okay?"

She turned at the sound of his voice—he could see that the left side of her face was raw and swollen—and she started to run toward him. "Keith, oh, Keith, it's so awful! They can't get Katia out!"

"What?" Keith suddenly went numb. He turned to look at the smashed-up car, which was surrounded by EMT workers. "My little sister's in there?"

"Yes," Victoria said. "But she's definitely alive. The EMT guys told me so. They just got the door of the car off."

"So she's going to be okay?" Keith demanded.

Victoria hesitated, biting her lip. "All they said was that she's alive."

Turning again to look at the car with its bashed-in door and shattered windows, Keith knew it was a small miracle anyone had gotten out of it alive.

Nikki Stewart felt totally content as she watched her boyfriend, Luke Martinson, strum his guitar. Her position as one of Hillcrest High's most popular students was guaranteed. The party she'd thrown that evening had been a complete and total success.

Well, actually, a few things *had* been a bit strange. For starters, Keith had pulled a mysterious disappearing act. More important, Suzanne had left early. Where had she gone so suddenly? And why? Nikki hoped she hadn't had a bad time. After all, Suzanne was the guest of honor.

Throwing a party for Suzanne was the very least Nikki could do for her new friend. If it hadn't been for Suzanne, Nikki wouldn't have been *going* to parties, much less *giving* them. In fact, she probably would be dead. . . .

The weekend before, Nikki had gone hiking with her two best friends, Deb Johnson and Victoria Hill, at Pequot State Park. Nikki had been furious with Suzanne at the time because she'd caught her and Luke kissing the night before, and Suzanne was the last person she wanted to see. Then when Suzanne had suddenly appeared on the same trail she, Deb, and Victoria were hiking, Nikki ran into the woods to get away. In her hurry, Nikki had stumbled and fallen into the rushing, swollen river just upstream from a dangerous waterfall. Suzanne had plunged into the freezing water, too, and pulled Nikki out just before she'd drowned. After that, the girls had made up and become even closer.

Nikki had managed to forgive Luke as well. After all, she had a guilty secret of her own. The same night she had caught Luke and Suzanne together, Nikki had almost kissed Luke's best friend, Keith, at the bowling alley. In fact, she probably *would* have kissed Keith if he hadn't pulled back. But that was all in the past now. She just wanted to forget about the whole thing.

Now it was nearing midnight, and the rowdy edge was off the party. Nikki's house had cleared out considerably. The people who were left had gathered into groups. The largest crowd was sitting on the floor in a semicircle around Luke, listening to him play his guitar and sing. Over by what was left of the food, John Badillo was entertaining some of the guys from the football team with his imitations of Coach Kostro. Deb Johnson was curling into one corner of the luxurious leather couch, deep in conversation with a girl from her biology class.

The doorbell rang. Nikki got up to answer it. But before she reached the door, it flew open. Ian Houghton rushed in.

"Ian, are you okay?" Nikki asked.

The handsome blond senior didn't *look* okay. He was pale, and he kept running his hands through his long hair.

Nikki sensed a crisis. She glanced at her guests, most of whom were gathering around her and Ian. Luke came to stand beside her. "Did something bad happen?" she asked Ian gently.

"I saw an accident on my way home," Ian said, trying to catch his breath. "I recognized Victoria Hill's car."

An image of her friend's body lying in the middle of the road flashed into Nikki's mind. She reached for Luke's hand.

"Was it bad?" Luke asked.

Ian nodded, looking miserable. "Pretty bad, I think."

John pushed through the buzzing crowd. "Victoria had an accident?"

Ian nodded.

"Did you see her?" John demanded. "And what about Katia? I asked Victoria to give her a ride home! *Did you see them?*"

Handsome, dark-haired John was the star

11

quarterback of the Hillcrest High football team. Nikki was used to seeing him calm and in control. But now, as he shouted out his questions in quick succession without giving Ian a chance to respond, John seemed to be coming unglued. And with good reason. Victoria was one of his closest friends, and Katia was his girlfriend.

"I didn't see Victoria or Katia," Ian said. "I just saw the car."

"Are you sure?" John demanded.

"Man, I'm sure."

Luke put his hand on John's shoulder. "Hey, calm down. We don't have any reason to think they were hurt."

"Well, I did see ambulances," Ian admitted reluctantly.

"Ambulances?" Deb squeaked out. "Oh, you guys, what if something terrible happened?"

Nikki put her arm around the pretty African-American girl. "Don't worry, Deb. I'm sure everything is going to be okay."

"Well, I'm going to make sure," John said. He grabbed his car keys and started toward the door.

"I'm going with him," Luke told Nikki.

Nikki's mind was whirling. Her friends could be hurt. They could even be dying. "Come on," she told Deb. "We're going, too."

"What about the party?" Deb asked.

Nikki looked around at the stunned faces of her guests. "The party is over," she announced.

She grabbed her purse and rushed outside, with Deb close on her heels. Luke and John were already climbing into John's car.

"You guys, wait up!" Deb yelled frantically.

As the girls squeezed into the tiny back seat of the black sports car, Nikki's heart started to beat faster. The night had grown foggy, and the roads were bound to be slick. . . . *Is John really in any condition to drive?* Nikki asked herself as he revved the engine. She hoped so. One tragedy was enough for the night.

Suzanne heard her mother's car pull into the driveway. She went to the kitchen door and waited for her to come in.

When her mother saw her standing there, she looked surprised. "Hi, honey," she said with a smile. "You're up late. How was the party?"

"Mom, I know."

Her mother put her purse down on the kitchen counter and slipped out of her jacket. Business as usual. "Know what?"

"I know about my father," Suzanne said, her voice rising. "Not only is he alive, but he lives right here in Hillcrest. He's my best friend's father, too!"

The color drained from her mother's face. "How did you find out?"

"I figured it out, Mom. There are lots of photos at Nikki Stewart's house. I'm not stupid, you know."

With a slight shrug, Suzanne's mother turned and started to unload the dishwasher, her hands noticeably shaking.

Suzanne stamped her foot. "Don't you dare ignore me! And stop acting like nothing is wrong!"

"Don't scream at me," her mother said.

"I'll scream if I want! And besides, who are *you* to tell me how to behave? First you lie to me my whole life, telling me my father is dead. Then when I find out he's alive, you tell me he doesn't know about me. And I probably wouldn't have found out that much if Victoria Hill wasn't such a huge gossip. And I really loved the fact that she knew the truth before I did. But that's not even the end of it. You swore to me you didn't know where my father was, and all the time you knew he was living a mile away! You are the biggest liar in the universe."

"I'm sorry."

Suzanne grabbed a plate out of the dishwasher and threw it on the floor. It shattered.

"Suzanne!" her mother said sharply.

"'I'm sorry' isn't good enough! Don't you even care that you've ruined my life?"

Her mother didn't answer. She'd started to sob.

Suzanne stood in front of her, clenching and unclenching her fists. "Please, Mom, just tell me the truth. The *whole* truth. Because if you lie to me again, I promise I'll hate you for the rest of my life."

14

Her mother sniffled and nodded. She wiped the tears from her eyes. "Okay."

Suzanne fell into a chair at the kitchen table.

Her mother sat opposite her. "It *was* Steven Stewart," she confirmed. "He was the one I fell in love with all those years ago. He was the one who left me to raise you alone." Her voice caught. "He was the one who broke my heart."

Seeing her mother so upset softened Suzanne's anger a little. "Why didn't you tell me?" Suzanne asked. She felt her own eyes begin to fill with tears. "I have a family I never even knew about—a father and a sister."

"*Half*-sister."

"Like that means it's okay to be strangers? We're still family," Suzanne insisted.

"Well, I don't think of them as your family!" Her mother's voice was harsh now. "How could I? How could *you?* All those years you suffered in poverty in Brooklyn, Nikki was being treated like a princess! She had things you never *dreamed* of having. And as for your father—he's a monster. The only way I could get a little piece of what we deserve, a little piece of what always should have been ours, was to promise not to tell a soul about his connection to us. He's scared of what will happen if his wife finds out."

Suzanne blinked. "What? Are you saying I can't tell Nikki she's my sister?"

"No, baby, you can't tell a soul," her mother said, leaning across the table toward Suzanne.

15

"If you do, you'll risk everything we have here. I might even lose Willis Workout." Ms. Willis's new fitness studio had become the hot place to exercise in Hillcrest. Even Suzanne's friends liked to work out there.

Suzanne leaned back, wanting to put more space between herself and her mother. Suzanne's head was spinning. Up until that moment she'd assumed that the pain she was feeling was worth it. At least she'd gained a father and a sister. But her mother was taking even that away from her. All she had gained was another painful secret.

"Suzanne, do you promise not to tell?"

"Mr. Stewart already knows I know."

"He won't tell. Will you?"

"I guess not," Suzanne said reluctantly.

"Promise."

"I promise," Suzanne whispered. *At least for now*, she added to herself. If her mother could lie, why couldn't she?

Two

John slowed his car to a crawl as he neared the accident site.

"Ian was right," Nikki said with a growing feeling of dread. "That's Victoria's car."

John pulled off the road and parked about fifty yards down from the ambulances. The four of them got out and walked toward a small crowd hovering near the side of the road. Several police officers were holding the people back. John strode quickly forward, but Nikki felt as if she were moving in slow motion. She was afraid of what she'd find when she got there.

As they neared the crowd, Deb grabbed Nikki's arm. "There's Victoria! I see her. She's all right."

"Do you see Katia?" John demanded tersely.

"No," Deb said.

They pushed toward the front of the crowd.

17

Nikki caught sight of Victoria. The back of one of the ambulances was open, and she was sitting just inside. Her face was bruised and cut, and her hair and clothes were a wet mess, but she didn't really look hurt—just very shaken. Still, something about her friend's posture told Nikki that everything was *not* okay.

"I'll be right back, you guys." Nikki bent down and crawled under the police barricade. As soon as she stood up on the other side, one of the officers grabbed her arm.

"Where do you think you're going?"

"Please let me go," Nikki pleaded. "That's my friend over there in that ambulance. I have to know if she's okay."

The officer studied Nikki's face, then let go of her. "Okay, go on."

Without a backward glance, Nikki rushed toward the ambulance. Victoria was sitting in the back all alone. She raised her head and smiled faintly when she saw Nikki approaching.

Nikki gave Victoria a tight hug. "We were so worried about you!" she exclaimed. "Are you okay?"

"I think so." Victoria seemed near tears. The enormous blanket someone had thrown around her shoulders made her look like a cold, scared little girl. "The paramedics said I have to go to the hospital and get my face checked out. Will you ride with me?"

"Of course."

Nikki sat down next to Victoria. Victoria rested her head on her friend's shoulder and drew in a shaky breath.

"Victoria, what happened?"

"This car practically came out of nowhere," Victoria said in a monotone. "If Katia hadn't warned me . . ." Victoria couldn't say what she was thinking. If Katia hadn't screamed out a warning, she wouldn't have swerved, and the other car would have hit them head on. Katia had actually saved her life.

"Where is Katia? Is she okay?" Nikki looked around hopefully.

Victoria's head shook against Nikki's shoulder. "She's unconscious. Keith is in the other ambulance with her. He drove up just after the accident. Oh, Nikki, it was so awful. . . ."

"Don't worry," Nikki said soothingly, wrapping her arm more tightly around Victoria. "Everything is going to be okay."

Nikki couldn't let Victoria know how panicked she was feeling. *Please let Katia be okay*, she begged silently.

Luke and Deb exchanged worried looks as John strained against the police barricade.

"Damn!" he muttered. "I can't see anything. What happened to Nikki? She said she'd be right back."

"Try to calm down," Luke suggested.

John didn't seem to hear him. He had turned

his attention to the police officer guarding the barricade. "You've got to let me through!" he demanded.

"I'm sorry," the officer told him. "That's an accident scene in there. Nobody goes through."

"But my girlfriend is in there! I have to see what's going on."

"You'd only get in the way," the officer said.

"She needs me," John thundered, straining forward again.

The police officer narrowed her eyes and looked hard at him. "Listen, kid, if you don't calm down, I'm going to arrest you."

Deb quickly stepped forward. "That won't be necessary," she told the officer. She put a restraining hand on John's shoulder. "Come on, John. The ambulance is about to leave. We can meet it at the hospital."

Luke gave Deb a grateful look. "Good idea. Come on, buddy. Let's go to the hospital. We can see Katia there."

"Well—okay," John agreed. He turned and started to push his way roughly through the crowd. Luke and Deb hurried after him.

In the ambulance Keith took a deep breath and forced himself to look down at his sister. He wasn't prepared to see her waxen face under an oxygen mask, the IV tubes running into her pale arm.

She looks dead, Keith thought in horror.

He knelt down next to the stretcher and took Katia's limp hand in his. "You're going to be okay, zeek," he said, using his own special nickname for Katia. "She *is* going to be okay, isn't she?" he asked the paramedic who was riding in the ambulance.

The man looked exhausted and sad. "If she's lucky."

After a quick ride, siren blaring the whole way, the ambulance arrived at the hospital. A group of doctors and nurses was waiting. Within seconds they had loaded Katia onto a gurney and rushed her down the hallway through a swinging metal door bearing a large sign that read No Admittance—Hospital Personnel Only.

Keith stood gaping at the sign, unsure of what to do next.

"You a relative?" a tall black man in hospital garb asked Keith.

"I'm her brother."

"Where are your parents?"

"At home, I guess. I—I don't think they know yet."

"Come with me." The man led Keith into a tiny glassed-in office and pointed to the phone. "Just tell them to get here. We'll give them the details when they arrive." The man slipped into the corridor and closed the door behind him.

Alone in the little room, Keith stared at the phone. *Don't think about it, just do it,* he told himself. Numbly he picked up the receiver and punched his parents' number into the phone.

His mother picked up on the first ring. "Hello?"

When Keith heard her voice, he closed his eyes and took a deep breath. "Mom?" Keith was surprised by how young and scared he sounded.

"Honey, where are you? It's an hour past your curfew, and your sister isn't home, either. Do you know where she is? Your father and I have been worried sick."

Tears pricked Keith's eyelids. More than anything, he wished he could tell his mother everything was fine. He wished he could change things so that he had never left the party early. Arrange it so he had been there to make sure his baby sister had gotten home safely.

"Is something wrong?" Keith's mother demanded.

He cleared his throat. "I'm at the hospital. Katia's been in an accident. You and Dad had better get down here."

"We're on our way."

"Oh, baby, are you all right? What happened to your face?" Victoria's mother rushed into the examining room where Victoria was resting. Victoria's father was not with Mrs. Hill.

Victoria turned toward her mother's concerned face. "I'm fine, Mom, just some cuts and bruises." She reached up and touched the gauze a young doctor had taped to her left cheek. "I just have to wear this overnight."

"What a relief!" Victoria's mother perched on the side of the high examination table where Victoria was sitting and gave her a gentle hug. "Darling, a police officer is outside. He wants to ask you a few questions. Do you feel up to it?"

"What does he want with me?" Victoria asked uneasily.

"It's just routine," her mother assured her. "He has to file a report on the accident."

"Okay," Victoria said quietly.

"I'll get him," her mother said.

As Victoria watched her mother walk out the door, she was filled with a sudden terror. What would she tell the police officer? That her own father was the drunk driver he was looking for? That this wasn't the first time her father had caused a car accident?

Victoria had been seven years old during that first horrible accident, and her relationship with her father had never been the same since that fateful day. After spending an afternoon at a family picnic, Victoria had chosen to ride home with her father. What a special treat, she had thought—just her and her beloved daddy on a nice ride home. Then the ride had turned ugly.

They'd been singing and laughing together when suddenly Victoria had heard a loud screeching sound and a bang . . . and then nothing at all.

Her father had hit another car.

As he'd quickly driven away, Victoria's father had assured her that everyone in the other car was okay. He'd begged Victoria to keep this a secret—their own special secret. And she'd never told.

But this time she couldn't keep quiet. She had to stop her father before he killed someone. She didn't care if he got arrested now. How could she care about him when Katia might die? She decided to tell the cop the absolute truth. Her father deserved whatever he got.

The door opened, and a police officer with pudgy red cheeks followed her mother back into the room. "Victoria Hill?" he asked crisply.

"Yes, that's me."

The officer gave her a businesslike nod. "Thanks for agreeing to talk to me. I won't keep you for long. I just need to know what happened tonight. Why don't you tell me about it in your own words?"

"We were driving down Harrison Avenue," Victoria said hesitantly. "It was raining really hard. Suddenly we saw a car coming from the other direction. It was weaving back and forth across the road." Victoria stopped, looked at her mother's concerned face, then took a deep breath. "The car crossed into my lane. I tried to avoid it, then everything went black."

"Did you see what kind of car it was?" the officer asked.

A red Jaguar. All Victoria had to do was utter

those words, and her father would get what he deserved.

Victoria's mother was smiling at her reassuringly. She wouldn't be smiling for long. . . . And, in a way, it would be Victoria who caused her mother's pain. She might never forgive her daughter for telling the truth.

Suddenly Victoria knew she couldn't do it. How could she tell the police it had been her father's car? Telling wouldn't ruin only *his* life; it would ruin her mother's, and her sister's, and her own.

Besides, even if the police arrested him, he would get out eventually. Victoria's father was often verbally cruel when he was drinking. He'd totally lost it when Victoria had been late to an important dinner, even though she had a good excuse. Then afterward he'd apologized for screaming at her and given her a gift—as if that made everything all right. Her jewelry box was filled with expensive jewelry he had gotten her to compensate for not being a good father. At that moment Victoria hated her father. But could she tell the truth and ruin his career?

The police officer was waiting, his hand poised above a little notepad.

"It all happened so fast." Victoria was avoiding the police officer's eyes. "I really didn't get a good look at the car." No matter how much she hated her father, she just couldn't destroy her entire family.

The police officer snapped the notepad shut. "I was afraid of that. Well, maybe your friend will remember something. I'll have to talk to her when she wakes up."

"*If* she wakes up," Victoria said glumly.

"It's a shame what happened to her," the police officer said. "But I don't want you to worry. We're going to catch this slimeball."

Victoria laughed harshly. "That would be great—right, Mom?"

Victoria's mother gave her a soothing glance. Then she calmly turned to the police officer. "My daughter has been through a lot. Is it all right if we go home now?"

"Sure," he said. "Thank you for your cooperation," he added as he left the room.

While her mother helped her into her jacket, Victoria's mind raced. What if Katia came to and identified her father's car? Her father would be arrested and brought before a court, and everyone would realize she'd been covering up for him. They might even have to move out of town. Of course, if Katia *didn't* make it, no one would ever know. . . .

"Can we see Katia before we go?" Victoria asked.

"Not tonight," her mother told her. "She's in intensive care. But don't worry, I'm sure she's going to be fine."

"I hope so," Victoria said. But she wasn't certain that was absolutely true. She felt awful for thinking it, but maybe it would be easier if Katia didn't make it.

When Keith came out of the consulting room where he and his parents had been meeting with Katia's doctors, he found Luke, Deb, and John waiting. They rushed forward to meet him.

"How's Katia?" John demanded.

Keith turned to his parents. "I'll catch up with you in a minute." They nodded and continued on toward the intensive care unit. Keith sighed as he watched his parents go. He was worried about them. His mother couldn't stop crying. And his father seemed a bit spaced out, as if he hadn't quite absorbed what had happened.

"Katia's in a coma," Keith told his friends.

"Oh, no," John breathed.

"How badly is she hurt?" Deb asked, holding on to John's arm.

"They don't know yet," Keith said. "They have to run a bunch of tests. Right now all we can do is wait. The doctors told us to go home and rest, but Mom wants to stay."

"How are you doing?" Luke asked Keith, his hand on his friend's shoulder.

"I—I'll be okay."

That was a lie, of course. Keith felt as if he were living a nightmare. The doctors had just told his family that Katia might never regain consciousness. How could he believe something like that? How could he accept that his little sister might die?

Three

"Victoria? You still asleep?"

Rolling over to face the wall, Victoria squeezed her eyes closed and did her best to ignore Nikki, who was calling to her from the hallway.

Nikki knocked softly on the door. "Vic? Can I please come in?"

Normally Victoria got up early. But it was already past noon, and she had no desire to get out of bed. Facing the day would mean facing the events of the night before. Why bother? Victoria asked herself.

The door creaked opened, and Victoria heard Nikki cross the room to her bed.

"Are you awake?" Nikki asked.

"No," Victoria said with a groan. "Leave me alone. I want to sleep."

"Please talk to me for a minute," Nikki pleaded softly. "I know it sounds silly, but I had nightmares all night. I just needed to make sure you're all right."

With a heavy sigh, Victoria opened her eyes and sat up. She didn't bother to push her sleep-rumpled hair out of her eyes.

Nikki sat down on a director's chair near the head of the bed. She was wearing a sweat-shirt way too big for her, and no makeup. She looked younger—and more vulnerable—than usual.

"What a night," Nikki sighed. "I feel like I hardly slept."

"Same here," Victoria said as she rolled her head from side to side. She had a dull pain in the left side of her face. Her neck and shoulder muscles ached, probably from the violent shock they'd received during the crash. She also felt grimy. The night before, she had been too upset to brush her teeth, wash her face, or change her clothes. Instead of wearing her luxurious silk pajamas to bed, she had picked a dirty T-shirt up off the floor.

"How are you feeling?" Nikki asked.

"Awful," Victoria replied.

Nikki chewed on her thumbnail. "You're still pretty shaken up, huh?"

Victoria closed her eyes and rubbed her forehead. "I think I have a right."

"Of course you do," Nikki said. "Listen, if you want to talk about it or anything, I'm here for you, okay?"

"Okay," Victoria said in a not-too-friendly voice.

"You know, I was pretty scared last night," Nikki went on. "When I saw your car on the side of the road . . . it was spooky."

Victoria's head snapped up. "Did my parents tell you about my car?"

"No," Nikki said with a surprised look. "I only saw your mom for a second. She was on her way to pick up Patricia at soccer practice."

"It's totaled," Victoria said with disgust. "The police called this morning to say they had to tow it away."

Nikki shrugged. "It's just a car."

"A one-of-a-kind car!" Victoria burst out, pulling the covers up to her chest. "It was worth a fortune, and now it's garbage."

Nikki reached out to touch Victoria's arm. "The important thing is that you and Katia are both alive. Forget about the car."

"I can't just forget about it!" Victoria said, shaking off Nikki's hand.

"Maybe your dad will lend you his car," Nikki said lightly. "That would be cool. His red Jaguar is totally hot."

"How could you say that?" Victoria exploded. "You know how I feel about my father. I don't even want to touch anything that belongs to him!"

Nikki seemed to shrink back in her chair. "I'm sorry. I didn't mean anything by it."

Victoria took a shaky breath. I've got to chill

31

out about Dad, she told herself. If I don't, Nikki will definitely guess something is up.

"I'm sorry," Victoria began. "I don't know why I'm giving you such a hard time. I guess I'm just worried about Katia."

Nikki scooted forward in her chair. "Anyone would be upset after what happened to you last night," she said carefully. "I was thinking that maybe you should see a psychologist—someone who can help you deal with your feelings."

Victoria almost laughed out loud. She could imagine that counseling session! First she'd tell the shrink her father was an alcoholic who had verbally abused her for years. Then she'd casually mention he'd recently taken it a step further and almost killed her with his car.

"I don't need a shrink," Victoria told Nikki evenly.

"Just a thought," Nikki said with a little shrug.

"A stupid thought," Victoria said.

"Okay, okay."

Victoria was relieved Nikki wasn't pressing the issue, even though she still looked worried. I wonder how she would look if she knew the whole truth, Victoria thought wryly.

She kicked off her covers and climbed out of bed. Crossing the room toward the big mirror over her makeup table, Victoria groaned. "Look at me!" she exclaimed. "I'm hideous."

Nikki came to stand behind her. "You have a black eye."

"No joke!" The skin around her eye had turned several dark shades of purple. Gingerly Victoria peeled off the tape that held a piece of gauze over her cut left cheek.

"It's not that bad—" Nikki started. But she was interrupted by an insistent beeping coming from the driveway.

"Now what?" Victoria groused.

Nikki ran to the window and looked out. "Wow! It's your dad, and he's driving an amazing car. I think it's a Porsche!"

Victoria shrugged without turning away from the mirror. "He bought himself a new toy. So what else is new?"

"What a beauty—it's a convertible!"

Beep! Beep!

Nikki turned away from the window. "Let's go down. Maybe he'll take us for a ride."

"No, thanks," Victoria said shortly.

"Why not?"

"Because . . ." Because what? Victoria asked herself. There's no believable reason in the world why I wouldn't want to see my dad's new Porsche—except maybe the truth. . . .

"All right," Victoria said with a sigh. "Let me just get dressed first." As she slipped into a pair of jeans, the girls heard the beeping again.

"Hurry!" Nikki urged her.

Let him wait, Victoria thought.

A few minutes later the girls came out onto the driveway.

"Good morning, Victoria," her father said with a big grin. But when he saw Nikki, he started to look uneasy. "I didn't know you were here, Nikki."

"Hi!" Nikki said brightly. "Great car! I love white Porsches." She giggled. "Of course, black ones are cool, too."

Victoria's father had regained his composure, and the smile was back on his face again. "Aren't you going to take your new car for a spin?" he asked, winking at Victoria.

Nikki's jaw dropped. "This car is for *Victoria?*"

"Sure," Mr. Hill said. "After what happened last night, I feel pretty lucky to have Victoria safe and sound. And since I had to get her a new car anyway, I figured she might as well have something special."

"Good thinking," Nikki said, still admiring the car.

Victoria's father casually approached his daughter, holding the car keys in an outstretched hand. "Here you go, Victoria."

Victoria felt like telling her father where to go and then throwing the keys back in his face. She knew exactly what he was trying to do. The car was just his latest bribe for her silence—bigger than the usual piece of jewelry because what he'd done was so much more horrible.

Nikki was watching Victoria with open curiosity. Victoria knew the fact that her friend was there had thrown her father. He'd probably planned to give Victoria this little peace offering in private.

Since Victoria made no move to take the keys, her father came closer and pressed them into her hand. He tried to put his arm around her shoulder, but she stepped away.

"Well, I hope you enjoy it," Mr. Hill said.

Victoria glared at him as he let himself into the house.

"I can't believe you," Nikki said when he was gone. "You didn't even thank him!"

"Why should I thank him?" Victoria asked. "He's just giving me what I deserve. Come on, let's go inside."

"Don't you even want to go for a ride?" Nikki asked.

"Nikki, I don't feel well, okay?" Victoria snapped. "If you don't want to come inside, then just go home."

"No, I'm coming." Nikki gave the car a final glance as she followed Victoria into the house.

Victoria didn't care if she never saw the thing again.

"Did you talk to Keith last night?" Nikki asked Luke on Monday morning. The two of them were sitting side by side on the back steps of school. Victoria was sitting on the step in front of them, staring straight ahead. The swelling on her face had gone down, but her left eye was still an angry purple. Deb was standing next to her, leaning against the handrail.

The first bell wouldn't ring for more than ten minutes. Nikki didn't usually get to school so early, but ever since the accident she had felt a need to be near her friends—especially Victoria. Whenever she thought about how close she had come to losing her . . . Nikki shuddered. She forced herself to concentrate on the here and now, and not start imagining horrible possibilities.

"Yeah, he called me from the hospital last night," Luke said, rubbing Nikki's knee.

"Is Katia any better?" Deb asked.

"Doesn't sound like it," Luke said. "She's still in a coma."

"Do they think she's going to make it?" Nikki asked.

"They don't know yet," Luke said.

"Can we visit her after school?" Deb asked. "I'd really like to see her."

Luke shook his head. "Nope. She's in intensive care and can't have any visitors except family. Keith and his parents have been there around the clock since Friday."

"Poor Keith," Deb said. "This must be horrible for him."

Victoria spun around to face them. "It isn't easy for any of us," she said sharply.

Nikki glanced at Deb, hoping she wouldn't take Victoria's tone personally. She was relieved when Deb nodded in agreement and said, "It's been terrible for everyone."

"Did Keith say anything about the police?" Victoria asked Luke as she twisted a lock of hair around her forefinger. "Are they any closer to finding out who was driving the other car?"

Luke shook her head. "Keith didn't say anything about that."

"I'm sure the police will find him soon," Nikki added, hoping to reassure Victoria.

"Well, don't be," Victoria said bitterly.

"But the police must—" Nikki started.

"Would you please wake up?" Victoria snapped. "This is real life, not TV."

"I didn't mean—"

"The cop I talked to didn't seem all that bright," Victoria interrupted again. "He probably couldn't find his own hand in the dark."

Nikki clamped her mouth shut. She wanted to be supportive, but she was dangerously close to losing her patience with Victoria. It seemed almost impossible not to offend her.

Deb cleared her throat. "Did you guys see what Sally Ross is wearing this morning?"

Nikki was pleased with the change of subject, and she shot Deb a grateful glance.

"Let me guess," Victoria said. "A long flow-ered skirt, a dirty tie-dyed T-shirt, white socks, Birkenstocks—oh, and a flower in her hair."

Deb giggled. "If she was wearing that, I wouldn't even mention it. That's what she *always* wears. Nope, this morning she was wearing black jeans, a black turtleneck, and a fairly cool flannel shirt. She was also hanging out on the ramp."

The year before, a ramp had been added to the rarely used front entrance of the school. The lower section couldn't be seen from the class-rooms above, so it had become a favorite hang-out for the kids who smoked.

"Are you sure?" Nikki asked. "Sally's not into that stuff."

"She's there on assignment," Deb explained. "She's planning to hang out with all of the differ-ent cliques at school and write about it for the *Chronicle*. The first article is the inside scoop on the ramp."

The *Chronicle* was Hillcrest High's student newspaper. Sally was one of the paper's most ac-tive—and most popular—reporters.

"That should be pretty interesting," Nikki said.

Victoria just shrugged.

Nikki's anger had passed. How could she be mad at Victoria when she'd almost died? And how could she blame her for being in a bad mood? She had every right to be shaken up. Nikki briefly wondered how Victoria would cope if Katia didn't make it, but then she pushed the thought out of her mind. It was too awful even to consider.

Suzanne spotted Nikki and the gang sitting together on the back steps. She walked toward them, her heart pounding in her ears. She hardly trusted herself to talk to Nikki now that she knew Nikki was not just her best friend but also her sister, her own flesh and blood.

Luke was sitting next to Nikki, looking very tired. Nikki had called Suzanne on Saturday morning to tell her about the accident. Luke was probably drained from a weekend of giving emotional support to Keith, who was his best friend. Still, in a faded blue shirt that made his eyes look even bluer, he was adorable. Suzanne felt a familiar tingle of jealousy. But it was even more intense and complicated now. She had even more reason to stay away from Luke. He wasn't just her friend's boyfriend anymore. Now he was her *sister's* boyfriend.

But it wasn't as simple as that. Suzanne had always been envious of Nikki and of the charmed life she seemed to lead. Now, for the first time, Suzanne felt as if she was entitled to everything Nikki enjoyed. Including Luke. As she drew closer, Suzanne wondered if she could get Luke away from Nikki if she really tried. It doesn't matter, Suzanne told herself firmly. You're not going to try.

"Hey, Suzanne!" Nikki yelled.

"Hey!" Suzanne felt herself smiling back, and it gave her a weird sensation. Did her smile resemble Nikki's? Did they look like sisters?

Suzanne sat down next to Victoria on the steps, but turned around so that she was facing Nikki and Luke. She tried to act normal as they filled her in on the latest about Katia and told her about Sally's project. Suzanne didn't give the conversation her full attention until Nikki announced that she had decided to audition for *West Side Story.*

She and Nikki were both in the drama club. So far the club hadn't done much, but that week things would move into high gear. Auditions had been scheduled for the fall musical. All the girls wanted to play Maria.

"I was thinking about trying out, too," Suzanne told Nikki. "But now . . . you know . . . maybe I shouldn't."

"Come off it," Nikki said. "Of course you should audition."

"You don't mind?"

"No," Nikki said. "I can stand a little competition."

Suzanne grinned. "In that case, may the best woman win."

"Do you want to practice together?" Nikki asked.

Victoria snorted. "The two of you helping each other practice for one part?" she asked, shaking her head. "How cozy." Suzanne knew Victoria didn't like her. She hadn't from the moment Suzanne and her mother moved to Hillcrest.

Nikki shrugged. "You know, if it weren't for Suzanne, I could be the one lying in the hospital hooked up to all those machines."

"That puts the school musical in perspective," Deb commented.

"It sure does," Nikki said, tossing her long blond hair over her shoulder. "I'd like to get the lead, but if Suzanne gets it, that's great, too. The important thing is that we're alive and that we're friends."

Victoria rolled her eyes.

But Suzanne was touched. "I'd love to practice my audition song with you. I'm sure you could help me a lot."

"And you could help me," Nikki said. "You're much better at staying on the beat than I am."

Suzanne smiled at Nikki. She was such a good friend. Nikki had even forgiven her for kissing Luke. Suzanne almost wondered if Nikki sensed she was more than a friend, if she somehow knew they were sisters.

Sisters. . . .

How am I going to keep such a big secret from my best friend? Suzanne asked herself. She wasn't sure she could.

"What can I get for you?" The hospital cafeteria worker pushed her glasses up with the palm of her hand as she waited for Keith's reply.

Keith blinked at her, trying to remember what he wanted. He was having a hard time thinking straight.

"You okay?" the woman asked.

"Yeah," Keith mumbled. "Give me two black coffees. No—make it three." Keith hated coffee, but he knew he needed a pick-me-up if he was going to stay awake.

As the woman moved about, preparing his order, Keith leaned against the orange and yellow counter. His eyelids felt swollen, and the smell of frying bacon made his stomach twist in protest. He hadn't been able to eat more than a few bites in the past three days.

Over the weekend Keith and his parents had spent as much time at Katia's bedside as the doctors would allow. The first time they'd seen her was near dawn on Saturday morning. The doctors fixed up her right shoulder and put that arm in a sling. They had also set a broken bone in her right leg.

The Steins had seen Katia three more times since that first visit. They'd all talked to her— Keith had told her a joke, Mrs. Stein had cried, Mr. Stein had sung Katia's favorite songs. But nothing made a difference. She hadn't responded; her condition had remained critical but stable. She looked as if she were sleeping peacefully, but Keith couldn't forget, even for a second, that his little sister was hovering near death.

He'd never been more scared in his life.

It's all my fault, Keith told himself for perhaps the thousandth time. If only I'd been a better brother. If only I'd taken care of her. If only I could change things. . . .

"Here you go, honey," the woman said.

"Thanks," Keith said. He handed her a five-dollar bill and pocketed the change she gave him.

It's strange, Keith mused as he picked up the tray. I've thought of Katia as a pain since the day she was born. And now that I know how much I love her, she may die.

Keith slowly made his way back to the intensive care waiting room—his new home away from home. When the Steins weren't with Katia, they were waiting to see her. Those hours were torture. Keith had flipped through every out-of-date magazine he could find and memorized the view from the windows there. It was impossible to sleep on those molded plastic chairs.

As he walked into the now-familiar room, Keith was struck by his parents' appearance. Their clothes were rumpled, their faces haggard from the strain. Keith's mother was wiping her nose with a shredded tissue; she had been crying on and off for days. Keith's usually formal father was slumped down in his chair.

Keith handed his parents their coffee. They took it without a word. Keith was wounded by their silence. They hate me, he thought as he fell into the chair next to his mother's. Who can blame them? If it weren't for me, Katia would be home and safe now.

As Keith took the first sip of his bitter drink, John strode into the waiting room. At the sight of his friend, Keith felt an unexpected surge of anger.

"Hi, Keith," John said uneasily.

"Hi," Keith replied without much enthusiasm.

Mr. and Mrs. Stein each gave John a weak smile.

John crouched down in front of Keith's parents and nervously ran his palms over his jeans. "How is she?" he asked.

"The same," Mrs. Stein said, staring into her coffee cup.

"But there's no brain damage," Mr. Stein added, slowly sipping hot coffee.

"But—but she's still in a coma?" John asked hesitantly.

Mrs. Stein nodded.

"Do they know how long she'll—be like that?" John asked.

"No . . ." Mrs. Stein sounded as if she was on the verge of tears, and Mr. Stein patted her knee.

Keith jerked to his feet and angrily motioned for John to come with him.

"We'll be right back," John told Mr. and Mrs.

Stein before following Keith out into the hallway.

"Really, how is she today?" John asked when they were out of earshot.

Keith was looking down at the floor, scuffing it with the sole of his shoe.

"How is she, man?" John persisted.

Keith finally met John's gaze. His eyes were hostile. "What do you care?"

"What do you mean?" John retorted. "I'm her boyfriend!"

"Her boyfriend?" Keith snorted. "You have a strange way of showing it."

"What's that supposed to mean?"

"Why didn't you drive Katia home on Saturday night?" Keith demanded.

"I—" John started.

But Keith didn't let him finish. "No, don't even bother answering that. I know why you didn't take her home. You wanted to stay at the party and flirt with the other girls. Well, let me tell you something—that's not love!"

John clenched his fists. "Who are you to talk?" he asked tightly. "I didn't notice you hanging around and making sure your sister got home safely. Where did *you* disappear to?"

"That's none of your business." Keith stepped closer to John.

John pushed Keith back. "If it involves Katia, it *is* my business!"

"That's enough!"

Both boys turned as a strong-looking, gray-haired doctor came striding down the corridor. Disgust showed on his face as he neared them.

"Just exactly what do you think you're accomplishing by behaving this way?" the doctor demanded. "Someone you love must be very sick or else you wouldn't be here. Trust me, your fighting isn't helping anyone."

Keith glanced down at the floor of the corridor, feeling like an idiot. How had he ended up almost punching out his sister's boyfriend, his friend?

"Keith." John held out his hand. "I'm sorry. I didn't come here to fight with you, man."

Keith hesitated for a moment, then reached out and shook John's hand.

"Thanks," John told the doctor.

"Everything okay now?" the doctor asked.

When both boys nodded, he continued down the hall.

"I'm sorry," Keith said quietly. "I shouldn't have blamed you. This isn't your fault."

"It's not yours, either," John said.

Keith tried to smile, and felt the tears he hadn't been able to shed up until that moment spill over. He'd never cried in front of John before, and he didn't know how his friend would react.

Awkwardly John threw an arm around Keith's shoulders. "Hey—it's okay."

"No, it's not!" Keith broke into gasping sobs. "I don't know what to do with myself. There's nothing I can do for her."

"Sometimes all you can do is wait," John said.

Wait, Keith repeated to himself. Somehow that was the hardest thing of all.

Four

Keith didn't know how happy he was to be back at school until he walked into the Hillcrest High cafeteria Tuesday afternoon. It was the usual chaotic scene: hundreds of kids eating, talking, studying—or doing all three at once. Keith was glad to get away from the oppressive atmosphere of the hospital, to be somewhere where sickness and death weren't on everybody's mind.

"Hey, look who's here!" Luke called as Keith neared the gang's usual table right in the middle of the cafeteria.

"Hi, you guys." Keith felt almost shy.

John was practically devouring him with his eyes. Clearly he was anxious for any news about Katia.

Nikki instantly sprang to her feet. She wrapped Keith in a warm hug. Normally Keith would have savored a hug from Nikki. Now he simply endured it for as long as he could and then pushed her away. It wasn't that he didn't appreciate her friendly greeting. He did. It was just that whenever anyone was nice to him, Keith felt as if he was going to break down. Keeping people at a distance was the only way he could hold himself together.

As he sat down Victoria reached out and touched his arm.

Keith hadn't seen Victoria since Friday night, and he was surprised by her black eye; she looked as if she'd been in a fist fight.

Suzanne and Deb gave him welcoming smiles.

"I'm surprised to see you," Nikki told him. "Are you sure you're ready to be back in school?"

"I'm positive," Keith said.

"How's Katia?" Deb asked, taking a bite of a green apple.

"She's still in a coma," Keith said. "But she's been moved out of the ICU. Though, there hasn't been any significant change since Saturday morning."

"When can we visit her?" John asked eagerly, moving even closer to Keith.

"Actually, I wanted to talk to you guys about that," Keith said. "The doctors say Katia might come out of the coma faster if she hears familiar sounds and voices. They want us to set up a schedule of times for people to visit."

"Sign me up," Deb said.

"Me too," Nikki added.

"Do you want me to come?" Suzanne asked. "I mean, I don't know Katia that well, but if it will help. . . ."

"That would be great," Keith said briskly. "But I have to warn you guys, Katia doesn't look that great. The thing is, this might be pretty tough. I don't want you to feel like you have to go alone. Sometimes it helps to have someone else with you." Keith glanced at John, wishing he knew how to thank him for having helped him through some difficult hours the night before.

Deb, Suzanne, and Nikki nodded seriously.

Victoria was staring into her yogurt. She seemed lost in her own thoughts.

"Sign me up for this afternoon, right after football practice," John said.

Keith cleared his throat. "The doctors said it would be good if everyone who's going to visit Katia stopped by the hospital sometime today. They'll have extra nursing staff around to answer questions and help everyone get used to the surroundings. We'll start the regular schedule tomorrow."

Everyone agreed, and Keith allowed himself a small smile.

Pulling a piece of paper out of his backpack, Keith blocked out a quick calendar and marked down the times his friends were available.

"I'm going over to talk to Katia's sophomore

friends," Keith announced when he'd finished.

"Need help?" John asked.

"Thanks, but no." Organizing visitors for Katia was the first useful thing Keith had done for her since the accident. He wanted to handle it himself.

Leaving his stuff with his friends, Keith crossed the lunchroom carrying his makeshift calendar and a pen. He stopped by a table of guys from the football team. Several of them were willing to help and had time to visit Katia. Keith marked them down on the calendar.

Leaving that table, Keith went directly to a group of Katia's girlfriends eating together. One with dishwater-blond hair was wearing a Mickey Mouse sweatshirt. She had braces on her teeth—the kind that connects the upper and lower jaw with tiny rubber bands. Keith recognized her from one of Katia's slumber parties over the summer. He knew her name was Diane.

As Keith approached the table Diane's eyes widened. She quickly whispered something to the other girls, and they all turned to stare at him.

"Hi. You're Diane, right?"

She nodded, then turned to her companions. "This is Keith, Katia's big brother." She introduced Keith to the other girls at the table.

"How is Katia?" a wispy-looking Chinese-American girl named Agnes asked.

Keith took a deep breath and explained about

his sister's condition. He told Katia's friends she needed visitors, then showed them his calendar.

"We don't drive," Agnes said. "How can we get to the hospital?"

Keith sat down and helped the girls figure out bus routes. Diane said her mother could drive them one afternoon a week. When that was settled, Keith started to fit the girls into the schedule. He'd already spent at least fifteen minutes at their table, and he was in a hurry to get away. Diane and her friends were annoying him. They kept looking at one another and giggling.

"Okay, I think we're all set." Keith was getting ready to leave when he noticed Diane's expression change.

He glanced behind him to find Victoria standing there. She was carrying his jacket and backpack.

"Lunch period is almost over," Victoria said, "and we're all taking off. Here's your junk."

"Thanks," Keith said.

"Why are you talking to her?" Diane asked loudly.

"What?" Keith asked, turning back to the table with surprise.

"Diane," Agnes said, a warning tone in her voice.

"I said, why are you talking to her?" Diane repeated.

"Victoria?" Keith asked. "She's one of my best friends."

"That's not what I heard," Diane said.

Whatever Diane's problem was, Keith expected Victoria to stand up for herself. When they'd dated the year before, she'd had no problem doing that. But when he glanced at her, he saw that her face had gone white.

Kids at nearby tables had turned around to see what the commotion was about.

"What do you mean?" Keith demanded of Diane. "How would you know who my friends are?"

"She was driving the car when Katia got hurt, wasn't she?" Diane said. "If I were you, I'd never talk to her again."

"That's right," said a red-faced boy from the next table. "If it hadn't been for her"—he pointed a skinny thumb at Victoria—"Katia wouldn't be in the hospital right now."

"You little creep!" Keith moved aggressively toward the boy. He would have hit him if Victoria hadn't stepped between them.

"It's okay," Victoria whispered to Keith. "Let's just go."

The bell signaling the end of the period rang, but nobody moved. Everyone was waiting to see what would happen next.

Keeping his eyes on Diane, Keith reached out a hand for his jacket. Victoria handed it to him.

"I want all of you to listen to me," Keith said quietly but forcefully. "I'm her brother, and no one is more upset about Katia than I am, but I don't blame Victoria for what happened."

"Why not?" The hotheaded boy hadn't calmed down yet.

Keith turned to him. "Because it wasn't her fault. Anyone could have been driving that car. The only person we should blame is the loser who ran Victoria's car off the road."

The speech seemed to have made an impression on Diane, who looked shamefaced. The boy had quieted down, too. Perhaps Keith had convinced him—or perhaps the boy was afraid of getting beaten up. Keith was a foot taller than he was.

Keith took his backpack from Victoria. He picked up his homemade calendar and stuffed it into his pocket. "I'll see you guys at the hospital."

Diane, Agnes, and their friends nodded.

Keith put his arm around Victoria. They walked out of the cafeteria together. "You okay?" he asked her.

Victoria nodded. "I'm getting used to it. People—certain people, at least—have been acting weird around me since yesterday."

"Well, they're stupid," Keith said quietly. "I'm just glad you weren't hurt."

Victoria smiled weakly. "Thanks. That's nice to know."

That afternoon Victoria hesitated in the hallway outside Katia's hospital room. Her courage had failed her. Naturally she had told Keith she'd visit Katia. Even though part of her was afraid of what would happen if Katia woke up, another part wanted to do everything possible to help her friend recuperate. But walking through that door and facing what her father had done to Katia . . . it was too much.

Nikki and Suzanne turned to see what was keeping her.

"What's the matter?" Nikki asked.

"I don't think I can go in there," Victoria whispered.

Suzanne gave Victoria a sympathetic smile. She looked a bit queasy herself.

But Nikki slipped an arm around her friend's shoulders. "There's nothing to be afraid of," she said. "It's just Katia in there."

Victoria let her breath out. "Okay, let's do it."

Nikki opened the door and led them into the room.

Katia had a private room, and the only sound inside was the hushed rasping of the various machines she was hooked up to. Brightly colored balloons were tied to the end of Katia's bed. The windowsill and bedside table overflowed with cards. Victoria's throat tightened when she realized Katia might never wake up and see this outpouring of love.

The girls slowly made their way to the bed. For a moment they stood looking down at Katia without speaking.

Nikki let out a shaky breath. "She's so pale," she whispered.

Katia was fair with auburn hair. Usually her flawless skin was one of her prettiest features, but now her skin had turned almost translucent. It had taken on the blue hue of the veins running below it.

A below-the-knee cast had been put on Katia's right leg; her right arm was in a sling. A small bandage ran across the bridge of her nose. Thin tubes ran into each of Katia's nostrils, and a fatter tube was taped into place in her mouth. Clear liquid was dripping into her veins through yet another tube, this one in her arm.

At the sight of her injured friend, all of Victoria's guilty feelings rushed out of the closed-away place she'd been keeping them in. She felt crushed by the enormity of what her father had done. How could she have covered for him? If Katia died, he would be a murderer. And she would be an accomplice.

Half blinded by hot tears, Victoria fumbled her way to the door. She couldn't control her feelings anymore.

"It's really kind of strange," Suzanne told Katia's still face. "I've been in town only a few weeks and already I've been to the hospital twice. The last time I was here was when Nikki almost drowned. . . ."

Suzanne let her voice trail off, and her eyes

flicked toward the door. She felt self-conscious. It was so strange talking to Katia when Katia never responded. Talking and talking without even knowing if Katia heard her. Besides, Suzanne wasn't at all sure Katia would care about hearing her voice. They'd only met a few times before the accident, and Suzanne had gotten the impression Katia wasn't particularly interested in being her friend. That was probably because Katia was so close to Victoria, and Victoria wasn't shy about showing how she felt about Suzanne.

Suzanne glanced toward the door again, but there was no sign of Nikki and Victoria. Nikki had run after Victoria when she'd fled the room in tears, and they'd been gone for at least ten minutes.

Suzanne's thoughts drifted to the last time she had been in the hospital. She hadn't known Nikki was her sister when she'd dragged her out of the raging river. Her sister. Suzanne's fury toward her mother rose again. How could she have lied to Suzanne about something so important? And how could she demand Suzanne keep this incredible information to herself?

Even though Suzanne had been hoping the door would open, she jumped up from the bedside chair she'd been sitting in when it finally did. She hastened to brush away the tears that were clinging to her eyelashes.

But it wasn't Nikki and Victoria. Instead Luke entered the room.

"Hi," Suzanne said, startled.

"Oh, hi." Luke glanced quickly around the room. When he realized they were alone, his eyes skittered away from hers. Seeing how uncomfortable she made him, Suzanne felt a stab of pain. But then Luke dared to meet her eyes, and Suzanne's sorrow deepened.

They hadn't been alone since the night they'd kissed. Suzanne found herself reliving the heart-pounding intensity of that moment. It was like an electric current running through her body, making every part of her tingle. It was the most exciting kiss she had ever experienced.

"Nikki's around here someplace," Suzanne finally forced herself to say. "Victoria freaked out earlier, and Nikki went to find her."

"Freaked out?" Luke still hadn't taken more than one step inside the door. He seemed frozen.

"I guess being at the hospital upset her," Suzanne explained.

"Lots of people hate hospitals," Luke said with a weak smile.

"Do you?"

Luke came closer and looked down at Katia from the foot of the bed. "Well, I guess you could say I'm used to them. Mom and I spent a lot of time here when my father was sick."

"That must have been horrible," Suzanne said, sitting back down in the chair by Katia's bed. She felt more comfortable now that they were actually having a conversation. But just being in the same room with Luke made her heart beat faster.

"My memories of that time aren't all bad," Luke went on. "Mom hadn't fallen apart yet. She was actually holding it together then, and the hospital staff were nice. I guess they felt sorry for me. I was just a little kid, and my dad was dying. They used to buy me presents and bring me candy and spoil me rotten."

"I bet you were a cute kid," Suzanne said.

"Adorable," Luke said with a smile. He pulled a chair up next to the one Suzanne was sitting in and gazed down at the girl lying in the hospital bed. "Hi, Kat," he said. "What's up?"

Suzanne was impressed by Luke's natural tone. Unlike Suzanne and the other girls, he didn't seem afraid of Katia.

Luke continued to address the unconscious girl. "Not feeling too good, huh? Well, I want you to do everything you can to get better, 'cause your brother's been real hard to get along with ever since your accident."

Tears pricked Suzanne's eyes as she listened to Luke. She had been teary ever since Friday night. Moreover, Suzanne felt as if she'd been on an emotional roller coaster for weeks. So much had happened so quickly that she hardly had time to take it all in. On top of everything else, the latest revelation about her father had totally turned her life upside down. Seeing Katia hadn't helped.

"Hey, don't cry." Luke reached for her hand as he turned to face her. He was so close Suzanne could smell the slightly familiar scent of his soap. She let herself go, crying even harder. The pain of losing Luke mingled with the hurt she felt from her mother's betrayal. Suzanne knew Luke was on the verge of wrapping his arms around her. She wanted to let him. She needed him so badly.

But then she thought of Nikki. It didn't matter how much she loved Luke. Her loyalty had to be to her sister.

Suzanne pulled her hand away. She stood up and wiped her eyes. "I think I'd better go."

"Are you sure you're okay?" Luke asked.

"Sure," Suzanne said with a firmness she didn't feel. "Listen, tell Nikki and Victoria I had to go."

"Okay," Luke said quietly.

Once Suzanne was safely out in the corridor, she let out a sigh of relief. It wasn't going to be easy for her to stay away from Luke, but she was determined to do it. For Nikki's sake.

Nikki sipped her tepid, bitter coffee and considered Victoria, who was sitting across from her at the table in the hospital cafeteria. She had stopped crying, but she was still moody and withdrawn.

"Do you want to talk about it?" Nikki asked carefully, afraid that Victoria would jump down

61

her throat. "It might make you feel better."

Victoria shrugged. She was tracing a pattern on the tabletop with her finger.

Nikki tried a different tack. "Remember how shaken up I was when I almost drowned? Coming that close to death . . . It was days before I could get it out of my mind, even for a minute."

"That's not it," Victoria said. "*I'm* fine."

"You're not feeling guilty about Katia, are you?" Nikki asked, suspecting that was the truth. "Because it absolutely wasn't your fault."

"No, it wasn't my fault," Victoria said, a strange look on her face. She didn't say anything more, but Nikki had an unshakable feeling that her friend was keeping something from her. She wondered if Victoria had told her the whole story of what had happened the night of the accident—or if she ever would.

Five

"Sally! Hey, Sally!" Deb yelled out in the lunch-room on Thursday.

"Must you shout?" Victoria asked irritably.

Deb ignored Victoria. She'd always been impossible, but in the days since the accident she'd been *extra* impossible. Deb was perfectly willing to cut her some slack—up to a point. She didn't see any reason why she shouldn't call out to Sally.

"Sally, over here!" Deb yelled again. The first article in Sally's newspaper series had appeared that morning. It was practically the only thing anyone had talked about all day at school, and Deb wanted to congratulate Sally.

Sally slowly made her way over to the table where Deb, Nikki, Victoria, and Suzanne were sitting. She was dressed in sweats and sneakers. Her frizzy hair was pulled up into a ponytail.

63

"Your article in today's paper is amazing!" Deb told Sally enthusiastically.

"It's no big deal," Sally said, but her delighted smile betrayed her true feelings.

"It is *so*," Nikki argued. "If I'd written something that good, I'd be sending it to the *New York Times*. You shouldn't be so modest."

Sally sat down in the chair next to Deb's. "Well, I asked the principal to change the name of the school to Sally Ross High, but he didn't go for it."

"I think schools are usually named after dead people," Suzanne said.

Victoria arched one eyebrow. "Sally Ross *Memorial* High School? Now that has a nice ring."

Sally blew Victoria a kiss.

Deb held in a sigh. Sometimes it felt as if she spent half her time listening to Victoria insult people she liked. "I thought your article was so funny," she told Sally. "The part called 'Smokers' Lingo' was great! I was reading it during French class, and I kept laughing out loud. I was afraid I'd get detention."

"I liked the part about Bill Moser," Suzanne spoke up. "He's in my history class, and I always thought he was kind of scary. Maybe because of all those heavy-metal T-shirts he wears—"

"Not to mention the combat boots," Nikki added.

"Isn't he the guy with the 'I Brake for Playboy

Bunnies' bumper sticker on his pickup?" Deb asked.

Suzanne nodded and made a face. "That's exactly my point. I always imagined I'd have zero in common with Bill. But Sally's article actually makes him seem like a nice guy."

"He *is* a nice guy," Sally said. "He reminds me a lot of Keith."

"Keith?" Nikki repeated. "*Our* Keith?"

Sally nodded. "They have the same sense of humor. They could be great friends."

"If they'd ever talk to each other," Deb said. "Which I doubt."

"That's your point, isn't it?" Suzanne asked Sally. "You're trying to get kids to be more accepting of people outside their own little group."

"I just report what I see," Sally insisted. "You can draw your own conclusions."

Suzanne smiled and shook her head.

"So what group are you going to profile next?" Nikki asked.

Sally stood up and struck a model's pose. "Guess. My outfit is a clue."

"The losers?" Victoria suggested sweetly.

"If that were the topic, I'd be dressing a lot more like you," Sally told Victoria with a wink.

"The jocks?" Suzanne guessed.

"Bingo!" Sally exclaimed. "For the next few days, I'm going to be a goddess of fitness."

Victoria snorted, but Sally didn't seem to notice. She waved good-bye to the other girls and started off across the lunchroom. Deb watched her go, and she would have sworn that Sally's walk looked more athletic. Hillcrest High's star journalist was already deeply involved in her next assignment.

"That's all for today, my little songbirds," Mr. Cadenza declared Wednesday afternoon in his lilting, Italian-accented voice. "We must not let our vocal cords become exhausted!"

Suzanne and Nikki exchanged amused looks. They were both fond of their music teacher's dramatic flair.

As the members of the chorus class started to make their way down the risers of the music room, Mr. Cadenza put his hands together in a beseeching gesture. "And please remember, auditions for *West Side Story* are in just two weeks. Those of you who will be auditioning—practice, practice, practice! Also, do not forget it is getting cold outside. Take good care of your vocal cords. Wear scarves. Keep your throats warm!" Mr. Cadenza was also the drama club's faculty sponsor. He would be directing *West Side Story*.

Nikki was shaking her head as she walked out into the hallway. "Mr. Cadenza sure has some crazy theories."

Suzanne smiled. "I don't know what modern medicine would say about it, but I'm planning to wear a scarf for the next two weeks. I'm not taking any chances."

"Have you decided what you're singing for the audition yet?" Nikki asked, falling into step beside Suzanne.

"I haven't decided, but Melissa told me she's singing 'Tomorrow' from *Annie*."

Nikki rolled her eyes. "Very original."

The girls stopped next to Nikki's locker.

"Did you pick a song yet?" Suzanne asked.

"I think I'm going to sing one of the songs Mr. Cadenza taught us in chorus," Nikki replied. "That way I won't waste time learning something new just for the audition, and I can concentrate on making it perfect."

"Hmm," Suzanne said thoughtfully. "That's an idea."

Nikki took out several books and then closed her locker with a bang. "Wanna come over and practice?"

"At your house?" Suzanne asked.

"Sure, where else?" Nikki gave her a puzzled look.

Suzanne was thinking about her father. She had been dreading the moment when Nikki would invite her over. She didn't know if she wanted to avoid him or spend more time with him. Her mother thought he was a monster. But he was still her father. She couldn't help being curious about him. Actually, the whole thing terrified her. She realized she wasn't ready to see her father again yet.

"I don't know . . . ," Suzanne began as they continued down the hall.

"I thought we agreed to practice together," Nikki said.

"We did," Suzanne said quickly.

"Don't tell me you changed your mind." Nikki seemed to be getting annoyed.

Suzanne stopped walking, closed her eyes, and rubbed her eyelids gently with her fingertips. "I haven't. It's just—"

"Katia, right?"

"Um—right," Suzanne lied.

"It's gotten to me, too. I was talking to my mom about that last night," Nikki said as they started down the hallway again toward their last-period classes. "She thinks it's important that we all visit Katia in the hospital. But she made me promise to keep up with the normal things in my life—like the musical. I think she has a really good point. Katia wouldn't want us to give up our own lives on her account."

"I guess not," Suzanne agreed. "Ah—my next class is in this room."

Nikki stopped walking and shifted her books to her other arm. "Let's get together on Saturday," she suggested. "That should give us enough time to decide what we're going to sing."

Suzanne thought of a way she could avoid her father. "Mom will be at the studio all day Saturday. Why don't we practice at my house? We'll have complete privacy."

Nikki wrinkled her nose. "But you don't have a piano at your house. We're going to need one." Nikki had a piano in her palatial bedroom.

Suzanne felt cornered. She considered asking Nikki if her father would be around on Saturday, but decided that would sound too suspicious. As she stepped out of the doorway to let someone into the room, Suzanne ordered herself to relax. Maybe Mr. Stewart—her father—wouldn't be at home. Then again, maybe he would. Suzanne wasn't sure which would be worse.

"So, what do you say?" Nikki asked as the bell rang.

Suzanne felt as if she had no choice but to give in. "Saturday sounds great," she said.

"Heading home?" Eric Shaw, a boy from Victoria's French class, asked her after last period on Wednesday.

"Yeah, I guess," Victoria said. Not that I'm in any hurry, she added to herself.

"Well, try to keep it under one-fifty," Eric said with a wink.

Victoria rolled her eyes.

That morning she had driven the Porsche for the first time. As much as she hated accepting her father's bribe, she *did* need a way to get around. She'd parked the car in the back of the student parking lot, hoping to avoid a scene. Fat chance. Of course, the Porsche had been noticed. She'd spent most of the day accepting compliments—and teasing—on it.

That same morning Victoria had finally gotten up the nerve to ask her father where his Jaguar was. It wasn't in the garage. She hadn't seen it since it zoomed away from the accident scene. Her father had coolly replied that it was in the shop for a broken fan belt. Yeah, right—he'd probably had the car towed to some repair shop west of the Rockies just to be sure the police wouldn't find it.

Victoria reached the student parking lot, but she didn't get into her car. Instead she kept walking toward the athletic fields. Having a game to watch would have been great, but it was too early in the season. All of the teams were still in preseason practices.

Without really thinking about it, Victoria found herself wandering down to the football field. She climbed up into the bleachers and sat down.

The afternoon was chilly. The sky was overcast with heavy gray clouds, and not too many people were watching football practice. Still, Victoria felt perfectly at home. She hadn't had any interest in watching football practice that year, but the previous fall, when she and John had been dating, she'd spent hours hanging out on the bleachers. She'd done her homework and worked on her tan while John learned the fine points of the game. After practice most afternoons, they'd gone to Pizza Haven and hung out until dinnertime. Victoria had to admit she missed those times. Maybe John and I weren't in love, she thought, but we had a good time together. And being the girlfriend of a football star certainly had its benefits.

Victoria's thoughts returned to Katia, and she felt a fresh wave of misery. Katia was John's girlfriend now. *She* should have been sitting there watching him run around and sweat. Instead she was in the hospital fighting for her life. Victoria considered getting up and going to the hospital. But she couldn't force herself to do it. She'd been there for the past two afternoons. She needed a day off.

Glancing down at the field, Victoria realized the girls' track team was making use of the track that encircled the football field. She picked out Sally Ross, who was huffing and puffing around the track while the real members of the team continually passed her. Victoria laughed out loud—so much for the fitness goddess!

She looked back at the football field and was surprised to see John. She'd assumed he would be at the hospital. Now she felt a little better about herself. Apparently even John needed some time away from that place. Maybe she wasn't so terrible after all.

"Hey, man," Mark, another part-time worker, greeted Luke as he walked into the Tunesmith on Thursday afternoon. The Tunesmith was a popular music store in downtown Hillcrest.

Luke worked there several afternoons a week as well as on weekends.

"Hey," Luke replied. He glanced around the store to see if his boss, Rick, was there. The door to the back office was open, and Luke saw Rick inside working at his computer.

Mark followed Luke's gaze and nodded. "Yeah, the boss is here. Three shifts in a row—a new record."

Luke felt a nervous twinge. Three shifts in a row . . . Did that mean Rick was beginning to suspect him? Luke's mother had lost her job and was sinking further and further into a deep depression. She was making no effort to find a new job. It wasn't as if they had savings to tide them over, either. In his desperation, Luke had started pocketing the money customers paid for CDs instead of ringing them up on the cash register. The previous week, though, Rick had noticed the inventory was off. Luke had quickly made up some lame excuse, but he wasn't quite sure if Rick had bought it.

Luke hadn't stolen any money since that close call, not only because he was afraid of being caught, but also because he had stopped believing the excuses he'd been making for himself.

I only did it because I needed the money, Luke reminded himself. It's just a loan till Mom gets another job.

Only they weren't loans. That was one of the little fantasies Luke had made up to make himself feel better. He wasn't even sure how much he'd taken, or how he could ever afford to pay Rick back.

"So, what are you in the mood for today?" Mark asked Luke. "Register or stocking?"

"What do we have to put out?" Luke asked.

"The new shipment came in from Columbia," Mark said. "Boxes are stacked up to the ceiling in the storeroom."

Luke had used his seniority to make sure he worked the register every shift for weeks—that was the only way he was able to get his hands on the money. He stared at Mark, feeling as if he was choosing much more than the afternoon's work.

"I'll stock," Luke said with effort. He held his hand out for the box cutter Mark was holding.

"Yippee!" Mark said with exaggerated delight. "I can't remember the last time I ran register."

"Have a ball." As Luke turned toward the storeroom his mood suddenly skyrocketed. It was as if he had broken some witch's spell in a fairy tale. He knew he'd never steal from Rick again.

Luke was actually humming as he cut open a box of CDs from some new British band called the Royal Bloodsuckers. But as he made room for the new releases on the rack, Luke felt the old doubts return. If he didn't "borrow" money from Rick, how would he and his mother pay the rent? Their landlord wasn't exactly a warm and caring individual. Luke knew there was a good possibility he and his mother would end up on the street.

It's not your responsibility, Luke told himself fiercely. As much as he wanted to hold his family together, he had to admit it was more than he could manage on his own. And maybe the extra money he'd brought home from the Tunesmith hadn't helped his mother at all. Maybe it had made it possible for her to sink deeper into her self-pity. Maybe she needed to hit rock bottom before she could pull herself together.

Still, Luke knew that letting his mother slide further would have some pretty nasty effects on his own life. If she couldn't pay the rent and they lost the apartment, he'd be out there on the sidewalk next to her. Luke forced that awful image out of his mind. It didn't matter what happened: he had taken his last dollar from the register.

When football practice ended, Victoria walked down to the field to say hello to John. She couldn't help smiling as he jogged toward her. He looked terrific in his practice uniform. The mud and sweat that covered his body only added to the effect. But when John took off his helmet, Victoria's pleasure faded. His eyes were red, and his face looked drawn.

"John, you look awful!" Victoria exclaimed.

He shrugged and gave her a weak smile. "I guess I haven't been sleeping much."

"Why don't you go home, take a hot shower, and then crawl into bed?" Victoria suggested. "You look like you're going to collapse."

John hung his head. "Keith's at the hospital now. I was thinking about heading over there before dinner."

Victoria bit her lip. "Yeah? I should probably go with you, but . . ." Her voice trailed off.

"But what?" John asked.

"I'm not sure I can deal with it this afternoon," Victoria admitted. "It's so hard, seeing Katia hooked up to all those tubes." Especially when I find myself wishing she wouldn't recover.

Victoria expected John to tell her she was being selfish. After all, it was his girlfriend who was lying there in a coma. But he only nodded and said, "I know what you mean."

Impulsively Victoria reached out and took his hand. "Listen, I think we both need an afternoon off. You can't do Katia any good if you have a nervous breakdown."

"Going home would be a waste," John said. "I know I couldn't sleep."

"Then why don't we go over to Hillcrest plaza, hang out for a while?" Victoria suggested. "I'll buy you some pizza."

"Yeah, okay," John agreed listlessly. "Whatever."

Victoria waited in her car while John showered and changed—it was their old routine. When he climbed into the passenger seat a few minutes later, she started the car and turned it toward Pizza Haven. Victoria felt relieved to have someplace to go and someone to go with. Anywhere was better than home.

It was still early for dinner, and when they walked into the restaurant, they found it practically empty. Victoria and John sat in their favorite booth near the back. Neither one bothered to look at the menu. They both knew it by heart.

The waiter came by and took their order for a large pizza with pepperoni and mushrooms.

Victoria raised her glass of diet cola in a toast. "Here's to an afternoon off."

But John refused to join in the gesture. "It's not really an afternoon off. I can't forget about Katia even for a second."

"I understand," Victoria said quickly. "That was a stupid thing to say."

John leaned over the table toward her. "Are you sure you don't remember anything more about that night? I'd feel a lot better if they nailed the creep who did this."

Victoria shook her head uneasily. She knew it was too late to start telling the truth now, but it wasn't easy to lie to John. "I don't remember a thing after seeing the headlights."

"You're sure?" John pressed.

"Yes." Victoria's throat was tight with tears.

John banged his hand down on the table. Their glasses of water jumped.

"It just doesn't make sense!" John exclaimed.

"If you saw the car coming toward you, why didn't you notice anything about it? Make, color—anything!"

"I don't know," Victoria choked out. "It was just so awful. Maybe I blocked it out." She blinked, and her tears spilled over. Even though her words were lies, the tears were real.

Victoria was so confused. She was afraid Katia would never wake up, and at the same time afraid she would. She was afraid to face her father. Afraid someone would find out the truth. And she was afraid her father would lose everything—that her family would be destroyed. The worst part about it was that she couldn't tell a soul. Not her best friend, Nikki. And not John—who stood to lose so much because of her irresponsible father.

"Don't cry," John said desperately. "You know I can't stand it when you cry."

But Victoria couldn't stop herself. The tears kept coming.

"Hey." John got up and slid into her side of the booth. He put his arms around her. "Shh, it's okay. Everything is going to be okay."

Victoria leaned her head against John's chest and felt herself calm down a little. There in John's arms, she almost believed everything *would* be all right.

Victoria raised her head and saw that John was crying, too. She'd never seen him cry before, and her heart ached for him. Victoria pulled

John closer, wanting to comfort him the way he'd comforted her. But as his face neared hers, Victoria experienced a surge of excitement.

Ever since school had started, while John dated first Suzanne and then Katia, Victoria had told herself she didn't want him anymore. But now that she was in his arms, she realized she had been lying to herself, protecting herself because he wasn't available.

Victoria moved even closer to John. When he didn't resist, she closed her eyes, and—

"Pepperoni and mushroom!"

Victoria's eyes flew open in time to see the smirking waiter put their pizza down.

John pulled away and nervously cleared his throat. "Let's eat."

Victoria smiled at him as he moved back to the other side of the booth. What an interesting afternoon. . . . She'd realized she wanted John back in her life—and now she planned to make him hers.

Six

On Friday evening Keith pulled into his driveway, sat in his Corvette, and stared up at the deserted house. He was supposed to go inside and fix himself dinner. Maybe even return some of the phone calls that had been pouring in from concerned relatives and friends. But he had no desire—or energy—to do any of those things.

Between his parents, the hospital, and the kids at school, Keith hadn't gotten away from thoughts of his sister for a second in the past week. Sometimes he felt like running away, going anywhere, just to get out of Hillcrest.

Suddenly Keith realized that this evening was his opportunity. His parents weren't expecting him back at the hospital. He was free to do whatever he wanted. Keith considered visiting one of his friends but quickly dismissed the idea. The instant he showed up, they'd get all serious—which wasn't what he wanted at all.

What, then? He didn't need anyone else to hang out with. He'd just go for a drive and see what he found. Already feeling better, Keith turned the car around and headed out of town on the highway. He abandoned himself to the sense of freedom the speeding car gave him.

About ten miles outside of Hillcrest, Keith spotted a billboard for some place called Pinewoods. That name rang a bell, but he didn't have time to read the sign before it whizzed by. It was several more miles before Keith realized why the name was familiar.

Pinewoods. The men in Mr. Martin's poker game had told him about the huge new casino located on a Native American reservation. The men had made the place sound like a class act. Too bad you had to be eighteen to get in.

Still, Keith didn't think anybody would mind if he just looked at the outside of the casino, so he took the next exit and followed the Pinewoods signs several miles down a newly paved road.

Keith felt disappointed as he pulled into the huge parking lot. The casino was a big, nondescript building that resembled a shopping mall.

I'll just peek inside, Keith told himself as he climbed out of the Corvette. Probably someone will demand my ID at the door.

But when he got to the door, nobody was

there. Keith stepped inside. It was like walking out of Kansas and into the Land of Oz.

The room was filled with motion and color. Dozens of bright, whirling slot machines were directly in front of Keith. Those are for old ladies, Keith thought derisively. But further in were the gaming tables surrounded by players, each with a pile of gaudy chips. Now that looks interesting. . . .

A beautiful woman dressed in a clingy red miniskirt approached Keith. He shifted his weight uncomfortably, knowing he didn't belong there and expecting the woman to demand to see his driver's license.

"Hi, honey," she said with a smile. "You look a little lost. Do you need some help?"

"I—well, it's my first time here. . . ."

"Welcome to Pinewoods," the woman said in a slightly bored voice. "Why don't you start with a complimentary drink at the bar?" She motioned to a long row of potted palms that separated the bar, which ran the length of the room, from the rest of the casino. "You can drink it at any of the tables."

Once Keith realized he wasn't going to be thrown out, his confidence returned. "I think I'll skip the drink," he told the woman. "Booze ruins my concentration. But I would like you to tell me how I can get into a poker game."

The blond woman showed him where to exchange his money for chips, and pointed out the poker tables. Keith changed his money, feeling thankful he was in the habit of keeping his entire stash on him. He did that because he couldn't risk having one of his parents discover it, but a side benefit was that he was always ready for action.

Carrying his chips, Keith headed toward the poker tables. He'd crossed only half of the noisy, crowded floor when someone clasped him on the shoulder. He spun around and found himself face to face with Tony, the bookie he'd met at Mr. Martin's.

"Hey, kid," Tony greeted him, his dark hair slicked back off his angular face. "It's nice to see you again. How's Lady Luck been treating you?"

Keith shook off Tony's hand. He hadn't forgotten the man's patronizing attitude the weekend before. "I don't rely on luck," he said coldly. "Now if you'll excuse me, a game of *skill* awaits."

"Don't let me keep you," Tony replied with a sly grin, brushing a speck of invisible lint from his dark suit.

Keith chose the table with the prettiest hostess—a tall brunette with flashing green eyes and long, shiny hair. Oddly, she reminded him a bit of Suzanne. He waited impatiently for her to deal him into the next hand.

When Keith finally picked up the cards, he felt his mood improving. This was just the medicine he needed.

He had crummy cards the first few hands,

82

and folded early. That was part of the game. The idea was to get out before any major harm was done and wait for better cards to come along. Half a dozen hands had gone by before Keith realized he'd been playing *too* conservatively. The dealer took a hand Keith could have won if he hadn't folded. Keith realized that while he had been playing, his thoughts had wandered to Katia, his parents, Tony, football. He'd lost over a hundred dollars without winning a single hand.

Keith tried to force himself to concentrate on the game. But the harder he tried to get back to even, the more money he lost. Whenever he had halfway decent cards, he bet aggressively. This new strategy only helped him lose more money more quickly. Soon his pile of chips had dwindled to nothing.

"Would you like to buy more chips?" the dealer asked.

"No, thanks," Keith said, reluctantly getting to his feet. He felt like a deflated balloon. He'd lost every hand. Now there was nothing to do but go home to his empty house or return to the hospital. Neither option appealed to him.

"Leaving already?" Tony called from the bar as Keith made his way to the door.

Keith was no longer unwilling to talk. What else did he have to do? He ducked into the bar area. "Yeah, I'm heading home," he told Tony.

"Would you like to join me for a drink?"

"No, thanks."

"So, did you have a good night?" Tony took a swallow of his drink.

Keith was tempted to lie, but he fought down the urge. "I had an awful night. I'm wiped out."

"Broke already?" Tony laughed, waving to the bartender.

"Well, I don't get a very big allowance." Keith wanted to show Tony he had a sense of humor, too.

Tony slapped Keith on the shoulder. "I tell you what, kiddo. I'm going to give you a loan."

Keith narrowed his eyes. "I don't want your money."

"It's a loan!" Tony said expansively. "You'll pay me back from your winnings. You don't plan to keep losing, do you?"

"No."

"So you'll pay me back!"

Keith glanced over his shoulder at the tables, feeling an almost physical need to return. He'd borrow a few bucks from this creep, win back what he'd lost, and repay Tony before he even left the casino. "Thanks," he told Tony. "A loan would be great!"

"Don't mention it," Tony said with a wink. Keith watched as Tony pulled out a large wad of money, peeled five bills off the top, and thrust them into Keith's hand.

Keith glanced at the money, expecting to see fifty dollars. It was five *hundred*. Keith raised an eyebrow.

"What's the matter, kiddo? Isn't that enough?"

"No, it's fine, thanks," Keith said. "You won't regret this."

"I know I won't," Tony told him with a smile.

At twenty minutes to one on Saturday afternoon, Suzanne parked her bicycle in the driveway of the Stewarts' lavish house. She took a deep breath and slowly let it out. She was early. Nikki wasn't expecting her until one.

The door of the garage was down, so Suzanne had no clue whether her father was at home. Actually, she didn't know whether she wanted him to be there or not. The whole situation was too weird.

Suzanne knocked lightly on the door. When it opened, her father was standing there. "Suzanne," he said with obvious surprise. "I—I didn't know you were coming over," he said awkwardly.

"Why would you?" Suzanne asked. You don't know anything about me, she thought.

Mr. Stewart smiled uneasily. "I guess I just thought Nikki would have mentioned it." He remained in the doorway, nervously shifting his weight from foot to foot.

"Mind if I come in?" she asked, surprised by how hostile her voice sounded. She had thought she'd feel more scared than angry. She hadn't planned to show her feelings, and she didn't realize until she was face to face with him how much she resented what her father had done.

"Oh, sure." Mr. Stewart forced a laugh as he stepped back.

Suzanne followed him inside. "Where's Nikki?" she asked, looking around the opulent house as if it were her first time there. Everything seemed different now that she knew this was her father's house.

"Upstairs in her room," Mr. Stewart replied. "But don't go up yet. I'd like to talk to you."

Suzanne hesitated. She was glad her father was showing some interest in her, but she was also terrified and confused. The man was a stranger to her. A stranger and yet her own father. He'd dropped out of her life for more than sixteen years. Now, suddenly, he wanted to have a little chat? Part of Suzanne felt like telling him off the way she imagined her mother had.

But was that really fair? Until recently he hadn't even known she existed. Besides, Suzanne was aching with curiosity. Who was this man? Was she like him? What was he thinking as he looked at her? Was he really as bad as her mother wanted her to believe he was? Maybe Suzanne should listen to his side of the story. . . .

"Okay," Suzanne finally said.

Her father broke into a grin. "Come on into the kitchen," he said. "I'll get you something to drink."

"Whatever," Suzanne said, trying to sound nonchalant and hoping he couldn't hear the pounding of her heart.

"So," her father began as he poured Suzanne a glass of diet soda, "how do you like Hillcrest?"

"What's not to like?" Suzanne asked sarcastically. "Except the fact that I don't fit in. See, all the kids here have always had everything they could ever want. It's pretty different from my life in Brooklyn."

Mr. Stewart handed Suzanne her drink and sat down across from her at the table. "Nikki told me you miss New York," he said, keeping his voice even. "She said you're very close to your grandparents."

"Of course I'm close to them. They practically raised me!" Suzanne didn't understand why she wanted to hurt her father so badly, but the desire burned inside her. "Mom worked two or three jobs, trying to make ends meet. It's not easy for a single parent, you know. If it hadn't been for my grandparents, *nobody* would have been there for me."

Mr. Stewart leaned across the table and reached for Suzanne's hand, but she snatched it away. "Suzanne, I know you hate me because of the way I turned my back on your mother. And I don't blame you. It was wrong . . . inexcusable. But I really did intend to go back to her."

Suzanne leaned back and crossed her arms. "So why didn't you?"

"I found out that my wife was pregnant, that I was going to be a father." He sighed deeply. "I couldn't divorce my wife when she was carrying my child, and I thought it would be easier to make a clean break with Valerie. I told myself that she would forget about me, find someone else. We were both young. It was only three weeks of our lives." Mr. Stewart paused. He sat perfectly still, staring off at nothing—as if he were watching a movie in his head.

Suzanne's heartbeat quickened. He looked so sad. Perhaps he really did regret what he had done. . . .

Suddenly Mr. Stewart snapped out of it. His eyes refocused, and he gave her a quick smile.

"Then, nearly seventeen years later, your mother came to visit me in the office," he continued. "I thought I was seeing a ghost. She was just as beautiful as ever. She told me about you for the first time, and I was horrified she hadn't come to me sooner. She was so strong and proud, so capable . . . I found myself falling in love with her all over again. I gave her the money to start Willis Workout, and I was glad to do it. Just like I'd be glad to give you anything you need."

He found himself falling in love with her all over again? Suzanne absorbed this new information with shock. Her mother had never hinted at that. . . . Did she even know? Suzanne felt her first flicker of sympathy for her father.

But wait a second, she told herself. What he was saying didn't square with what her mother had told her. He had to be lying.

"That's a very romantic story. Too bad I know that's not the way it happened. My mother told me she had to force you to give her the money. She said that when she threatened to tell your wife you had another family, you panicked."

Suzanne's father's face turned bright red. She half expected him to have a heart attack on the spot. But then he sighed and gave her a sad smile.

"I don't know what your mother told you—or why—but you're here in Hillcrest because I wanted you near me. I'd like nothing better than to introduce you to the world. You and Nikki, my two beautiful daughters, are my pride and joy."

"So why don't you do it?" Suzanne demanded.

Mr. Stewart banged his fist on the table. "Because of your mother! She's not exactly a forgiving woman. How can I risk what I have for someone who won't even give me the time of day? Who wants to destroy me? I'm nothing but a bank account to her." Suzanne's father laughed bitterly. "And I still love her. I must be crazy, but I get dizzy whenever I see her."

Suzanne began to wonder if her father was actually telling the truth. He seemed so sincere. And she wanted to believe him so badly.

He leaned toward her across the table. "Suzanne, if you could just convince her I'm not the enemy. . . ."

Suzanne allowed herself to imagine a happy ending to her personal tragedy. Her mother would forgive her father, the two of them would get married, and everyone would live happily ever after.

It sounded like a fairy tale. But would it *really* be a happy ending? What about Nikki? How would she feel if her parents got divorced and her father married Suzanne's mother? Rotten, obviously. And betrayed. Nikki might never even speak to her again. The truth was that Suzanne's mother and father had created an awful mess all those years earlier. It was too late for a happy ending. Suzanne couldn't help hating them both for that.

Nikki turned off her stereo and listened to the voices coming from downstairs. One was definitely her father's. Who's Daddy talking to? Nikki wondered.

She got up and padded out into the hallway. Her bare feet didn't make a sound as she walked down the back stairway that led directly into the kitchen.

At the bottom of the steps, Nikki stopped. She was stunned by the sight that greeted her: her father talking to Suzanne. Clearly this was not small talk. They were sitting together at the kitchen table, heads close together, talking in low, intense voices.

Nikki cleared her throat.

Suzanne and her father glanced up. They looked surprised, which irritated Nikki. Why should they be surprised to see her in her own house?

"I didn't know you were here," Nikki said to Suzanne, a note of accusation in her voice.

Suzanne quickly stood up. "I just got here. Your father offered me something to drink."

Nikki's father didn't move from his place at the table. He was avoiding her gaze. What could he have been telling Suzanne in such an intimate, urgent way? Sometimes her father was so busy he didn't have time to exchange two words with her, and yet he had taken the time to talk to Suzanne. Why?

"So, are you ready to rehearse now?" Nikki asked in a testy voice.

"Sure," Suzanne said nervously. She put her glass in the sink and joined Nikki on the steps.

Nikki led the way up the stairs. As Suzanne followed her she found herself wondering how she was going to keep all this a secret from Nikki.

Nothing in the world is more satisfying than a good shopping trip, Victoria told herself as she kicked open her bedroom door on Sunday afternoon. She had just gotten home after spending hours at the mall with her sister and mother. They'd hit practically every store.

With a grunt, Victoria heaved a collection of

multicolored shopping bags onto her bed. She noticed the red light on her answering machine was blinking. She had three messages.

Not only do you have the hottest new clothes, Victoria told herself, you're popular! Flopping down on the bed, she reached out and hit the playback button. While the tape rewound, Victoria kicked off her sandals and started to search through her shopping bags for the incredible deep red nail polish she'd just purchased. She had seen the color in a magazine and was dying to try it.

Here it is . . . first the toes, then the fingers, Victoria decided. Humming to herself, she opened the top drawer of her bedside table and started to look for her polish remover.

Beep. "Vic, this is John. Are you there? Please pick up if you are."

Victoria's good mood vanished into thin air. As she listened to John's anxious voice, her throat tightened up. He sounded as if he had some tragic news to announce. Now what?

After a long pause, John's message continued. "Okay, well, I guess you're not there. It's late Sunday afternoon. Give me a call when you get in."

Victoria reached over and turned off the machine. The other messages could wait. Tossing down the nail polish, she grabbed her thin black cordless phone and quickly punched in John's number. As reluctant as she was to deal with yet another problem, she was psyched John had turned to *her* for help.

The phone rang four times before John picked up and mumbled a gloomy hello.

"Hi, it's me. I just got your message. You okay?"

John sighed deeply. "Not really."

Victoria's fingers went numb with fear. Was it possible Katia had woken up and identified her father? Was John calling to break the bad news?

"Whatever it is, you can tell me," Victoria said, fighting to keep her voice steady. "What—what's wrong?"

"What isn't?" John said in a dead tone.

"Did you see Katia today?" Victoria asked carefully.

"No. That's just the problem. . . ." John's voice trailed off.

She's dead, Victoria thought. Daddy really killed her!

John took a deep breath and continued. "I had football practice all day today. I was planning to come home, hop in the shower, grab a quick bite, and then go over to the hospital. But I fell asleep at the table. Mom didn't even wake me up."

"So what happened with Katia?" Victoria asked.

"I didn't wake up until past visiting hours," John said. "I didn't get to see her all day."

"But she's not any worse?"

"No. I called the hospital, and they said there's been no change."

"And she didn't wake up?"

"No—I wish!"

Victoria slumped onto her bed and let her breath out in a rush. Along with her relief came a generous portion of irritation. Why had John worried her over something so insignificant?

"I feel like I'm letting Katia down," John said. "I should be there for her every day. I'm thinking about quitting the football team so I'll have more time to spend at the hospital."

"What?" Victoria could hardly believe what she was hearing. "You're thinking of giving up football—the most important thing in your life?"

"It's not as important as Katia," John said.

Victoria shook her head. This was unbelievable! If it hadn't been for the accident, John would have been bored with Katia by now. He'd probably be thinking of a nice way to dump her, not moping over missing a chance to see her for an hour. Victoria took a deep breath and tried to think. John was losing it. She had to talk him out of ruining his life.

"I'm letting Katia down," John repeated.

"You'd be letting her down if you quit the team!" Victoria exclaimed.

"Do you really think so?" John asked.

"I know so," Victoria said. "If—*when* Katia wakes up, she'll feel terrible if you've given up the most important thing in your life because of her."

"I don't know. . . ."

"Besides," Victoria said delicately, "you have to think about what will happen if she *doesn't* make it."

"No!" John said. "I don't even want to think about that."

"I'm sorry," Victoria said soothingly. "I shouldn't have said that. But believe me, when Katia gets better, she's going to want to see you out on that field doing what you do best."

"Okay," John said. "If you really think it's what Katia would want, I won't quit. Because she *is* going to be okay."

"I'm sure she will be," Victoria agreed.

But she wasn't sure. And the more time she spent with John, the less she wanted Katia to recover. Not just out of fear for her father, but because ever since the afternoon at Pizza Haven when she'd felt John's arms around her again, Victoria had become painfully aware of how much she missed him.

Now she was convinced John needed her, too. Moping over Katia wasn't healthy for him. All Victoria had to do now was remind him just how happy he could be—with her.

On Sunday evening Suzanne sat in her room staring at her history book. But she wasn't really seeing the words on the page. Instead she was hearing her father's words ringing in her head. "I found myself falling in love with her all over again."

What if that was true? What if her father wasn't someone to be hated, but rather someone to be pitied? Imagine living the life he had. Losing the woman you loved while you were barely in your twenties. Being married to someone else and having a daughter with her. Spending all those years trying to forget. And then—bang! Your true love steps back into your life and makes you realize all the happiness you've missed.

My parents should get back together again, Suzanne decided.

But if they did, Nikki's parents would have to break up. . . .

Ever since Suzanne had spoken to her father on Saturday afternoon, she'd been unable to think about anything else. Her rehearsal with Nikki had been a joke. After an uneasy and unproductive hour, Suzanne had made an excuse and left. She'd spent most of the last day and a half alone in her room, trying to figure out how she felt about her father, whether she wanted to let him into her life.

Now Suzanne decided she had to *do* something, or else she'd go crazy. She slammed her book closed and got to her feet. She had to be sure her mother knew Steven Stewart still loved her. Maybe it wasn't too late for them to be happy. Her father had asked her to convince her mother he wasn't the enemy. Well, she was willing to give it a try. After all, what did she have to lose?

Suzanne found her mother lounging in bed, reading the newspaper. She was wearing an old sweatshirt and her chunky reading glasses. Suzanne hesitated in the doorway. Maybe it wasn't the best time to approach her mother. She looked exhausted, and Suzanne knew she had put in a long day at the studio—not only dealing with business but also teaching some of the most strenuous aerobics classes.

But her mother had already noticed her. She put down the paper she was reading and pushed her glasses up into her hair. Suzanne figured her mother was probably surprised to see her. In the week since she'd learned her mother had been keeping her father's identity a secret, Suzanne had been avoiding her.

"Hi," Suzanne's mother said tentatively. "How's the homework going?"

"Not so good," Suzanne admitted, taking a few steps into the bedroom. "I can't concentrate."

Her mother smiled weakly. "I guess that doesn't really surprise me. You have a lot to think about."

"Mom," Suzanne said, crossing the room and sitting down on the edge of the bed, "I saw Dad yesterday."

"Oh." Her mother's mouth tightened with disapproval.

"I can't help seeing him," Suzanne said defensively. "Nikki's my best friend. And besides, I *want* to know what he's like."

Her mother shrugged slightly. "If you decide that's something you want to do, I can't stop you. I just imagine it must be awkward. Doesn't Nikki think your interest in her father is a bit unusual?"

"I don't know," Suzanne admitted. "Probably. But I don't care. Mom, he told me something I think you should know." Suzanne paused. There was no turning back now. "He said he still cares about you. Actually, he said he was in love with you."

"And you believe that?" her mother asked. No smile. No delighted look.

"Why not?"

"Listen, Suzanne, I don't know what kind of fairy tales your father has been spinning for you, but I want you to get one thing straight. All I want from him is financial help. Period. Once my business is off the ground, I don't want to have anything to do with him. And I don't want anyone to know I ever did."

"But Mom, he *loves* you," Suzanne argued. "How can you ignore that?"

"It's not hard after what he did," her mother said, sounding tired. "Nobody has ever hurt me more deeply. I could never trust him again. And I can't help thinking he's just sweet-talking you the way he once sweet-talked me."

"You don't believe he really cares about me?" Suzanne asked, her voice breaking.

"I didn't say—"

Suzanne jumped to her feet and strode out into the middle of the room. "Our relationship is entirely different than yours was. Don't forget that!" she said, her voice rising. "I'm not like you were—some babe he was trying to get into bed. I'm his *daughter*."

"Suzanne," her mother said too calmly, "I know how much it must mean to you to find your father—"

"If you had any idea," Suzanne interrupted, "you wouldn't have kept him a secret my entire life!"

"I thought I was doing the best thing for you," her mother said.

"Well, if you ask me, you're just trying to put all the blame on him." Suzanne pointed a finger at her mother. "You're not so sweet and innocent, you know. You've lied to me since I was born. I'm not sure *I'll* ever trust *you* again!"

With that, Suzanne fled back to her room and slammed the door. Tears of frustration were running down her face. How could her mother suggest her father was using her? She was the one who was the liar. Suzanne was certain her father was telling the truth. And she was just as certain how he felt about her. She didn't care what her mother thought. She planned to spend as much time with him as she could.

*   *   *

99

Luke followed the familiar hospital corridor past the nurses' station and into Katia's room. Keith was already there. He had pulled a chair up close to Katia's bed and was reading to her. Luke was thankful Mr. and Mrs. Stein were nowhere around. The two of them were turning into some kind of sleep-deprived zombies. Luke hoped they were off somewhere getting some rest.

"Hey," Luke greeted his friend.

"Hi," Keith said, putting the book down on the bedside table.

"How's she doing today?" Luke asked, looking more at his best friend than at Katia.

"No change," Keith said, sounding defeated. "She's been like this for so long, I can't even imagine her waking up anymore."

Luke felt a chill. Keith was beginning to sound depressed. Luke knew all the signs— thanks to his mother.

"Don't talk like that," he told Keith. "She's going to get better. I thought you said the swelling in her brain had gone down."

"That's what the doctors say," Keith told him. "But I don't know—she looks the same to me."

"Well, I'm sure the doctors wouldn't lie," Luke said. "If they say she's getting better, it must be true."

Keith didn't reply, and Luke desperately tried to think of something to say that would cheer his friend up. Finally it came to him.

"Did you see your name in the *Chronicle* today?" he asked.

"No," Keith said flatly.

Luke slipped his backpack off his shoulder, unzipped it, and sifted through the contents. "Here it is. You're mentioned in Sally Ross's article. Do you want to read it?"

Keith shrugged. "Maybe later."

"Why don't I read it out loud?" Luke suggested. "I'm sure Katia would enjoy it, too." When Keith didn't protest, Luke cleared his throat and started to read.

DON'T KNOCK THE JOCKS
BY SALLY ROSS

What do you think of when someone says the word jock?

Probably you think of the slim physique of John Badillo, Keith Stein, or one of the other golden heroes who led our football team to victory last season. Well, at least that's what I always think of.

An embarrassed grin brightened Keith's face. "That's not bad. Sally makes me sound like some kind of stud."

"I told you you'd enjoy this," Luke said, wiggling his eyebrows. He turned back to the article and picked up where he'd left off.

So it was with visions of glory that I planned my week as a jock. Naturally, my first choice was to hang out with the football team (see above). But with the big season opener approaching, Coach Kostro told me to . . . well, he said no. So I ended up joining the crew on the river for practice Monday at 5:30 A.M. (That was me in the back of the scull with the Dippin' Donuts bag.) After school I joined the team for aerobics and weight training. I finally got home just as my family was sitting down to dinner. I hadn't realized how, er, different I smelled until my mother stood up and yelled, "Who let the skunk in here?"

Keith laughed out loud. "My mom always says I smell like an elephant after football practice."

"You do," Luke said.

Keith picked a plastic cup up off the bedside table and threw it at Luke.

Luke deftly ducked, and the cup missed him. He went back to reading. Sally's article described the rest of her week: running with the track team, volleying with the tennis team, and jumping up and down with the cheerleaders. She talked about the joys of sore muscles, shin splints, bruises, and dumb-jock jokes. Keith smiled through the whole thing.

"Guess who she's profiling next," Luke said.

Keith shrugged.

"A group she calls the Prom Queens," Luke said.

"In other words, your girlfriend," Keith said.

Luke nodded. "Yup, Nikki and Victoria and Deb—maybe even Suzanne."

"I can hardly wait," Keith said. "That should be very interesting."

Luke was pleased to note that his friend didn't sound the least bit depressed anymore. But as he looked at Katia his satisfaction faded. Keith wouldn't be okay until she was okay—and that might mean never.

Seven

On Tuesday of the following week, Suzanne went back to Nikki's house. Officially she was there to practice her audition piece. Her real mission was to see her father. She was determined to get to know him better. She had been the one to suggest the second practice session at the Stewarts'. In fact, she'd talked Nikki into it.

"That was beautiful," Suzanne told Nikki after she'd listened to Nikki run through the Rodgers and Hammerstein song she'd chosen to sing.

Nikki made a face. "If you really think so, maybe I'd better get someone else to practice with."

"What do you mean?"

"I was behind the beat for the entire second verse," Nikki asserted. "Don't tell me you didn't notice. You have perfect rhythm."

105

Suzanne fiddled with the sheet music in front of her on the piano. Her mind *had* wandered while Nikki was singing. She was disappointed because her father hadn't been home when they'd arrived. But just after Nikki had started to sing, Suzanne had heard a car door slam in the driveway, and from that moment on, Suzanne's ears were attuned to any sound that would confirm that her father was in the house.

Nikki was watching her suspiciously, and Suzanne did her best to pull her attention back to their rehearsal. Spending time with Nikki had been bittersweet ever since Suzanne had learned Steven Stewart was her father. Keeping the truth to herself was driving her crazy.

As much as Suzanne longed to tell Nikki the incredible fact that they shared the same father, she was also afraid of what would happen if she did. How would Nikki react? The only way to find out was to tell her. But what if she got mad or freaked out? It would be too late for Suzanne to take it back. And even worse, her new-found father might get angry as well and shut her out.

"I'm sorry," Suzanne told Nikki. "Why don't you run through it again? I promise to give you my complete attention this time."

Nikki hesitated. "Suzanne, what's going on? For the last week or so, I've felt as if you were about a million miles away."

"Oh, I'm fine," Suzanne said quickly.

"If you don't like practicing with me, that's okay," Nikki said.

Suzanne laughed. "I love practicing with you. So come on, sing!"

"Why don't you take a turn?" Nikki asked with a sigh. "After that last run-through, I could use a break."

"Okay." Suzanne stood up and waited while Nikki settled herself on the piano bench. Nikki played the piano much better than Suzanne did, and her ability really came in handy.

Nikki hit the opening chords of Suzanne's song.

Suzanne started to sing from memory. The song she had finally chosen was a lush, romantic ballad. She found it impossible to get the right emotion into her voice while staring at the top of Nikki's head, so she closed her eyes.

She threw everything she had into the song—belting out the words and striving to hold the last note as long as possible. As Suzanne finished, she heard applause. Her eyes flew open. Her father was leaning against the door frame, clapping and beaming at her.

"Daddy!" Nikki exclaimed. "Don't sneak up on us like that! Did it occur to you that Suzanne might not want you eavesdropping on her singing?"

Suzanne felt the blood rush to her face. "It's okay. I don't mind."

"That was beautiful. You're really very talented," Mr. Stewart said to Suzanne.

"Thanks," Suzanne whispered. Her heart thudded as she studied his handsome, open face. She wondered if she was beginning to love him.

"Daddy, do you mind?" Nikki asked sourly. "We're trying to practice."

"I'm sorry, sweetie," Mr. Stewart said. "But I just wanted to see if you girls were getting hungry."

"You did?" Nikki asked incredulously. "Where's Mom?"

"Working late," Mr. Stewart said. "So I thought the three of us might go out to dinner together."

"It's a school night," Nikki reminded him.

"Oh. Do you have a lot of homework to do?"

"Yes," Nikki said.

"No," Suzanne said at the same time. She was surprised by how heartless Nikki was being to her father—*their* father. Couldn't she hear the disappointment in his voice?

"We have to eat something," Suzanne pointed out.

"Well, I guess," Nikki said grudgingly.

Mr. Stewart grinned in delight. "Then it's settled. Now, where should we go?" he asked, sounding like an excited kid. "Oh, I know!" he exclaimed before they had time to reply. "We'll go to the Arboretum. I can already taste their grilled tuna."

"The Arboretum?" Nikki repeated. "What's up, Daddy?"

"I just feel like celebrating," he told her.

"Celebrating what?" Nikki asked.

"Sometimes you don't need a reason to celebrate," he said, winking at Suzanne. "Now if you girls are finished practicing, let's go. I'm starved."

"I'm ready," Suzanne said. She picked up her sheet music and stuffed it into her book bag.

"I want to brush my hair," Nikki groused. "I'll be ready in a minute. Do you think you can wait that long, Daddy?"

"Absolutely," Mr. Stewart replied. "I'll be downstairs."

Suzanne flopped onto Nikki's bed and watched her friend fuss with her hair. In spite of Nikki's crabby mood, Suzanne felt terrific. Her father wanted to have dinner with her! That could mean only one thing: He was as anxious to get to know her as she was to get to know him.

"Your menu, miss," the tuxedoed waiter at the Arboretum said politely.

"Thanks," Nikki said without enthusiasm.

"I don't know how I'll ever decide what to order," Suzanne bubbled. "Everything sounds delicious." She turned her brilliant smile on Nikki's father. "It was so nice of you to suggest this."

Nikki thought Suzanne sounded ridiculously grateful. After all, her father was just taking them out to dinner. It was no big deal.

But Mr. Stewart looked pleased. "The food here is excellent."

"I know." Suzanne giggled, sounding to Nikki like a baboon on laughing gas. "I've actually been here before."

"With your mother?" Nikki's father asked.

"No, on a date," Suzanne told him, looking around the beautifully decorated room. "A disastrous date."

Now Nikki's father started to laugh. "Uh-oh. Poor guy. I bet you broke his heart. I guess you already know all the gory details, huh, Nikki?"

"I've heard the story." To Nikki's ears, her own voice sounded cold. She didn't even know why she felt so grumpy. Well, she had some idea. The way Suzanne got along so well with her father positively irked her. Nikki's dad had never once shown this much interest in any of her other friends. In fact, he was always forgetting Luke's name—even though she'd been dating him for two years. For that matter, her father had never once invited Luke out to dinner. His interest in Suzanne was totally bizarre.

Or was it? Nikki realized her father actually had a very good reason to be nice to Suzanne: She had saved Nikki's life. He was probably just showing his gratitude. Nikki felt a flash of guilt. *She* was the one who should have been showering Suzanne with gratitude. Instead she was begrudging her a dinner out.

"I'm going to have the duck," Nikki said

brightly, setting her menu down on the white tablecloth with a decisive thump. She decided she'd do her best to be pleasant. "It comes with these incredible garlic mashed potatoes."

"Sounds low-cal," Suzanne said with a wink.

Nikki's father laughed loudly.

Nikki shot him a look. Suzanne's comment hadn't been *that* funny.

The waiter returned. "Are you ready?"

"I'll have the tuna," Mr. Stewart told him.

"The same for me," Suzanne said. "It sounds delicious, *and* it won't blow my diet."

Mr. Stewart smiled as if Suzanne had discovered the cure for cancer. "Good choice."

"I'll have the duck," Nikki said through gritted teeth. Although she knew she didn't have to worry about her weight, Suzanne's little comments had made her feel like a hog.

The waiter took away their menus and hurried across the carpeted floor.

"So, Suzanne." Nikki's father turned to face Suzanne. "You seem to be enjoying yourself here in Hillcrest."

Suzanne beamed. "Oh, yeah. It's so different from Brooklyn. It's so clean and quiet . . . and I've made tons of friends."

"That's wonderful, dear. And you're doing well in school, I assume." He was talking to Suzanne as if he found her to be the most fascinating person in the world.

"So far, so good." Suzanne giggled.

111

And Mr. Stewart laughed out loud.

What's their problem? Nikki wondered as she tuned out the conversation. Dad's acting like I'm not even at the same table, and Suzanne's totally loving all the attention.

Nikki could feel the resentment boiling up inside her. Suzanne may have saved her life, but she had also horned in on it in a major way. First she'd come on to Luke. And now she was monopolizing the attention of Nikki's own father. Gratitude was all well and good—but how much did Nikki have to take?

Luke suppressed a sigh as he yanked a grocery cart out of the long line of carts in the front of the store. The refrigerator at home contained one moldy orange, a half-eaten can of tuna fish, and some flat soda. A week had passed since Luke had vowed to stop stealing from the Tunesmith—and his wallet contained exactly fourteen dollars. This shopping trip was going to call for some serious creativity on his part.

He maneuvered his cart around a harried-looking woman who was trying to convince two small boys they didn't really need *another* box of candy, and paused next to the apples. Ninety-nine cents a pound. Luke picked up a glossy red apple and tried to guess how much it weighed. Too tricky, he decided, placing it back on the stack. He pushed his cart toward the pasta aisle.

In the past week, Luke had tried to let all of

the responsibility he'd been shouldering slide back onto his mother. Over the weekend his mother had actually done a sinkful of dishes and accepted a call from the landlord. Luke had almost believed she was going to pull herself together. But Monday after school he'd found her passed out on the couch—and she hadn't left the apartment since.

Luke had just thrown a couple of boxes of pasta into his cart when he spotted Suzanne pushing an almost full cart toward him. He broke into a wry smile. He'd never seen any of his other friends in the grocery store. They all probably sent their maids.

"Hey, Luke!" Suzanne called, waving at him.

"Hi!" As Luke watched Suzanne approach he marveled at how similar she was to Nikki in so many ways—the same shapely legs, the same kissable lips, the same perfectly arched eyebrows. It was as if they'd been cut from the same pattern, but using two different kinds of cloth. Which one is prettier? he asked himself. He didn't know the answer, but he did know which one he'd been thinking—and dreaming—about lately.

"What's up?" Suzanne dragged her cart to a stop next to him.

"Just a little shopping," Luke replied.

Suzanne frowned at the contents of Luke's cart. "That sure is a *little*. My mother left me a list about a mile long."

113

Luke licked his lips and tried to act cool. That wasn't easy, since just being near Suzanne raised his temperature about a thousand degrees. He pretended to be interested in the food she'd chosen. "A gallon of ice cream—no, *two* gallons? Frozen pizza, bread, eggs, potatoes . . . You and your mom really know how to eat."

"Yeah, well, Mom's always starving. All those aerobics classes, you know. And I can't get through my French homework without something sweet." A smile slowly spread over Suzanne's face. "We had a blast at lunch today— where were you?"

"With Keith." Luke knew no further explanation was necessary.

"Oh, I should have guessed. Well, Sally Ross sat with us—she's working on an article about our crowd." Suzanne paused, and her face turned a delicate pink. "Well, not exactly *my* crowd. It's more your crowd—yours and Nikki's and Deb's and Keith's. But Sally insists the rest of the school thinks I'm part of it, too."

"You are," Luke said firmly.

Suzanne looked delighted. "Sally asked us all sorts of questions about being part of the quote-unquote popular crowd. She asked Victoria how she liked having guys hanging all over her, and Victoria said"—here Suzanne stuck her nose up in the air and spoke in a snotty tone—"'I'm sure you'll never know.'" She giggled. "I was actually relieved Victoria had someone else to pick on for once."

"Mmm-hmm," Luke murmured. He was having a hard time concentrating on what Suzanne was saying. He was too busy thinking about how she *looked*—and he thought she looked as if she wanted to be kissed.

"Well," Suzanne said. "I guess I'd better get going. Ice cream, remember?"

Was it Luke's imagination, or did she seem reluctant to leave?

"Okay," he said softly. "See you."

As Suzanne pushed her cart down the aisle, Luke couldn't stop his eyes from following her. The attraction he felt for her was becoming impossible to ignore.

"John?" Victoria paused with her hand on the door of Katia's hospital room.

John was the only visitor in the room. He was sitting in a chair next to Katia's bed, slumped forward, his head in his hands.

Victoria crossed to him, her cowboy boots clicking loudly on the tiled floor. "John? Are you okay?"

John slowly raised his head and ran his fingers through his thick dark brown hair. "Victoria, hey, how are you doing?"

Victoria crouched down next to John, taking one of his powerful hands in hers. She hated to see him so upset.

"Better than you seem to be doing," she told him.

John's lips twisted into a distant-looking smile. "Do you realize it's been almost two weeks since the accident?" he asked. "All that time Katia has been just lying here. I've probably spent two entire days talking to her, pleading with her to wake up. And—nothing! Nothing makes a difference!"

"Shh . . ." Victoria laced her fingers though John's.

Knowing what she was about to do, Victoria felt a tiny twinge of guilt. Katia might have been unconscious, but her presence still filled the room. Memories of the happy times she and Katia had shared raced through Victoria's mind, but she quickly pushed them away. Though Katia was her friend, it didn't change the fact that only one of them could be John's girlfriend.

Forget about Katia, Victoria urged herself.

Suddenly John jerked his hand away from hers and smacked it against the arm of his chair. "Why won't she wake up?"

"John, come on, snap out of it." Victoria reached for John's hand again, brought it up to her lips, and kissed it. "Getting upset like this isn't going to help."

"Sometimes I wonder if anything will," John said.

Victoria stroked John's cheek. "There's nothing you can do," she whispered.

"No," he said mournfully.

"There's nothing anyone can do," Victoria

whispered. "You just have to let go." As she spoke she cautiously stood up and leaned close to John. Then she kissed him ever so gently on the lips. Victoria slowly pulled away a fraction of an inch and waited for his reaction.

For a moment neither of them moved. Victoria could feel John's warm breath on her face. Her heart thumped painfully. Then John grabbed Victoria and passionately returned her kiss.

He wants me as much as I want him, Victoria thought with satisfaction as she savored his embrace. Any guilt she'd felt faded away. She slipped into John's lap, not caring that they were making out in Katia's hospital room or that anyone could walk in and see them. All she cared about was the delicious warmth of John's body as it pressed against hers.

"Excuse me, sir," Nikki said in her best annoying-customer voice. "Could you please recommend a good CD? And none of that nasty rock and roll. That junk hurts my ears."

Luke looked up from the cardboard box he was cutting open and smiled at Nikki. He stood up and gave her a quick kiss on the cheek. "What are you doing here?"

Nikki sighed. "Some greeting. Don't overwhelm me with enthusiasm or anything."

"Hey, don't get so defensive," Luke said in a tone Nikki didn't like at all. She felt her spirits, which had been hovering around her knees, crash all the way down to her toes.

"I'm not being defensive," Nikki said in a crabby voice. She'd spent most of that afternoon in the house, feeling rotten. Part of her bad mood came from never seeing Luke anymore. He was always with Keith at the hospital or working. She'd thought this visit to the Tunesmith would cheer her up—but it was having just the opposite effect.

"So what's up?" Luke asked in an obvious attempt to change the subject. "Has Sally been giving you the third degree?"

Nikki frowned. "How did you know about Sally? I don't remember telling you about it."

"Suzanne told me," Luke said.

"Suzanne?"

"Yeah, I ran into her at the grocery store last night," Luke said.

"Why didn't you tell me?" Nikki asked suspiciously.

"Why would I?" Luke asked. "It wasn't any big deal."

Nikki took a deep breath and did her best to calm down. Why was she getting on Luke's case? He hadn't done anything wrong. Nikki reminded herself that Luke was *her* boyfriend. He loved *her*. So what if he talked to Suzanne at the grocery store? That was innocent enough.

"I'm sorry," Nikki said, letting her breath out in a big rush. "It's Suzanne. She's driving me insane."

Luke was watching her closely. "I thought you two were friends."

"We are. It's just—" Nikki hesitated, feeling strangely nervous. She didn't want Luke to disapprove of what she had to say. She took a CD off the rack and fiddled with it. "It's just that Suzanne is everywhere lately. In my classes, eating lunch with me, everywhere. I bet Sally's article will be all about her."

"Why is that such a big deal?" Luke asked.

"It's not," Nikki said. "I'm just bugged. Suzanne's been practicing her audition song over at my house almost every afternoon. And my dad is totally into her. It's so weird. They're like buddies . . . or no, I know what it is—it's like he's adopted her or something. Or she's adopted him, actually. I mean, why can't she look for her own father and leave mine alone?"

"I think you're overreacting," Luke said. "Your dad's probably just grateful to Suzanne because she saved your life."

"Oh, and you think I should be grateful, too, right?" Nikki demanded hotly. "Well, my gratitude tank is just about empty. I don't owe her anything more."

Luke shrugged. "Give Suzanne a break. You don't know what it's like, not having a father."

"Oh, I get it. You do, so that makes you and Suzanne two of a kind. Great, Luke. That's real cozy."

Luke didn't say anything. He also didn't

bother to hide his disgust. Nikki realized she was in danger of losing more than just a few hours of her father's attention. She found herself wondering about the night she'd caught Suzanne and Luke kissing on the golf course. She was finding it harder and harder to believe that it had really been a mistake, as they'd claimed.

Nikki forced a smile. She was such a crazy mix of emotions. She just needed to be alone and sort this all out. "I'm out of here," she told Luke as evenly as she could.

"Are you okay?"

"Yeah. I'm sorry if I'm acting weird. I'm just in a terrible mood."

"Don't worry about it. I'll call you when I get home."

"No, don't," Nikki said. "I'm going to bed early."

Luke reached for Nikki's hand and pulled her close. He kissed her forehead. "Take good care of yourself tonight. And remember, I love you."

Nikki felt tears fill her eyes. Luke's words were comforting, but something in his desperate tone told her he knew their relationship was unraveling, just as she did.

I've got to hit the books tonight, Keith told himself as he walked down the hospital corridor toward Katia's room. Starting with math.

Coach Kostro had bent his rules for John and

Keith, allowing them to miss practice occasionally to visit Katia. But the principal had held firm on his rule about student athletes having a C average: maintain it or sit on the bench.

Keith had to work hard to get C's when nothing was on his mind but football and school. With all of the added stress he'd been dealing with lately, keeping up with his studies was a real struggle. *I wonder if a teenager can have a heart attack?* Keith thought as he passed the nurses' station. *If so, I'm a likely candidate.*

He pushed open the door to Katia's room and stepped inside.

Katia's friend Diane was standing near the window, her arms crossed. When Keith came in, she spun around and glared at him. Her expression quickly softened. "Oh—it's you. Hi, Keith."

Keith suspected Diane had a crush on him. The skinny sophomore didn't turn him on at all—the two years between them felt more like twenty—but flirting with her gave him a major ego boost.

"Hey, Diane. Who were you expecting? Your boyfriend, maybe?" As he spoke Keith dropped his backpack on the yellow vinyl chair and crossed to Katia's bed.

"Don't I wish . . . Katia looks a little better today," Diane commented.

Keith stared down at his sister's face and asked himself if that was true. The cut on the bridge of her nose was healing. And she was less pale . . . maybe. Keith's mother had convinced herself Katia's color was returning. She'd re-peated the observation so often, Keith wondered if she'd brainwashed him into believing it.

"Yo, zeek." Keith forced himself to address Katia even though his face heated up when he did. He hated speaking to his sister with other people in the room.

To cover his embarrassment, Keith glanced up and winked at Diane. "So, who were you expecting earlier?"

A shadow crossed Diane's face. "I was afraid— Well, I thought it might be *her*."

"Who?"

"Victoria Hill," Diane said with disgust.

Keith groaned. He felt like shaking Diane. Why did she insist on blaming Victoria for the accident? He'd told her *he* didn't blame Victoria. That should have been enough to make her drop it.

"I told you before, Victoria is one of my best friends," Keith said, his voice much less friendly. "I'm really not into listening to you insult her."

"But—" Diane started.

"I don't want to hear it!" Keith exploded.

Diane turned to stare out the window, which looked out onto the hospital parking lot. She was chewing on her bottom lip; tears were flood-ing her eyes.

Keith was in no mood to deal with a crying girl—especially one he didn't like very much.

"I'm sorry," he mumbled, biting back his irritation. Why don't you just go home? he added to himself.

"Please don't hate me," Diane said in a tortured voice. She was still facing the window. "It's just that I . . . know something about Victoria."

"What's that?" Keith asked in a disinterested tone.

Diane slowly turned around. "Yesterday my friend Agnes was here. Remember Agnes?"

"Yeah," Keith said impatiently. He was searching through his bag for his math book, only half listening to Diane's shaky voice. Her presence was beginning to annoy him big-time.

"Well, when Agnes came into the room . . ." Diane paused to take a deep breath.

"What?" Keith demanded. "If you have something to say, say it!" And then get out, he thought.

"Fine!" Diane's voice was shrill. "She saw your *friend* Victoria kissing Katia's boyfriend!"

Keith froze. For a second his mind refused to absorb this information. It can't be true, he told himself. Victoria and John kissing . . . here? In Katia's hospital room? The thought of it made Keith sick.

"Are you sure it was John?" Keith whispered, still staring into his backpack.

Diane laughed harshly. "Believe me, every girl at Hillcrest knows exactly who John Badillo is. Agnes knows what she saw."

Why shouldn't I believe it? Keith asked himself. Victoria and John had been all over each other ever since they'd first hooked up. Their passion hadn't cooled even after they'd stopped dating. Keith himself had seen them making out the week after Victoria had dumped John for cheating on her. Why would anything change now?

Keith had been worried all along that John would break Katia's heart. Of course, he'd never dreamed she'd be in a coma at the time. . . .

Keith studied Diane's flushed face, and a new thought burst into his brain. Could Diane have made this up? She hated Victoria. Maybe this was her way of getting revenge.

"Whatever Agnes saw," Keith said evenly, "I'm sure it was all innocent."

"Innocent?" Diane repeated with an uncertain frown.

"Don't spread this story around," Keith warned.

"I won't," she replied, her voice small.

"Why don't you take off now?" Keith asked.

"I don't have to go yet," Diane said. "My mom isn't coming to pick me up for another half hour."

"Wait for her downstairs," Keith said firmly.

"But—"

"I said *wait for her downstairs!*"

Diane's mouth dropped open. She rushed around, gathering up her jacket and books. At the door she paused and looked back. "I just want you to know I didn't make this up," she said. "And neither did Agnes."

As the door swung noiselessly closed behind Diane, Keith let out a ragged sigh. All he could do was hope Diane was the liar, and not two of his best friends.

After Nikki left the Tunesmith, Luke tried to relax and enjoy the rest of his shift. That shouldn't have been too difficult. Since he'd quit· stealing from Rick, his guilt had lifted somewhat, and Luke had started to like work again. He loved listening to new CDs the minute they arrived from the record company, and he even liked creating order out of the chaotic shelves. Most of his coworkers were pretty cool, too.

But that day the rest of Luke's shift was pure torture, because Rick was hanging around "helping." Rick was in a foul mood. He'd snapped at a customer who asked too many questions and yelled at Adele, an older, dark-haired part-timer, because she came back late from her break.

"What's wrong with Rick?" Adele whispered to Luke when their boss was safely out of earshot. "He's usually such a pussycat."

"Beats me."

"I hope this isn't a new management style or anything like that," Adele said with a worried frown. "If he lays into me like that one more time, I'll quit."

125

After the way Luke had taken advantage of Rick, he felt protective of him. "Cut him some slack. Maybe he had a fight with his girlfriend or something."

Adele grinned. "Maybe his boat sprang a leak."

Rick's passion for his boat was a joke among his employees. At one time or another, all of them had been trapped in his office while he displayed snapshots of *High Fidelity*, his beloved speedboat.

"If something happened to the boat, you know we would have heard about it," Luke said.

Adele giggled. "And heard about it, and heard about it."

The door of Rick's office banged open. "Luke!" Rick called. "Would you come in here? I'd like to talk to you for a minute."

Groaning, Luke got to his feet and made his way toward the office. "What's up?" he asked Rick.

"Close the door," Rick said with uncharacteristic sharpness.

As Luke complied, his heart started to pound. Rick knows I'm a thief, he told himself. But when Luke turned around and saw his boss's troubled face, he knew at once that Rick wasn't angry. He looked upset.

"Is something wrong?" Luke asked, propping himself on the edge of the chair in front of Rick's desk.

Rick was slumped way back in his chair. "I don't want you to repeat what I'm about to tell you."

"Okay," Luke agreed.

Rick pulled himself up and leaned forward. "I went over the inventory records last night. The stock is way below where it should be."

"I don't understand," Luke lied. He knew exactly what Rich was talking about. "Do you think we have a shoplifting problem?"

"No," Rick said quickly. "I thought of that, but our security system is top-of-the-line. I'm afraid someone is cheating us, someone who's part of the Tunesmith team."

"Oh." Luke was afraid to say anything more. If by some chance Rick didn't know he was guilty, Luke didn't want to say anything to give himself away.

"I was wondering if you had any idea who it could be," Rick said.

"Why are you asking me?" What Luke really wanted to ask was, Do you suspect me?

"Because I trust you," Rick said. "You work here almost as many hours as I do. Of all my part-time employees, you seem the most dedicated."

Relief washed over Luke. But he didn't let his guard down. "I wish I could help you," he said. "But the truth is, I can't imagine anyone who works here stealing."

Rick sighed and rubbed his eyes. "Neither

can I. That's the problem. Well, thanks. Maybe it will turn out to be some kind of massive computer error."

"I hope so," Luke said, and he left the office.

Luke slowly sat down in front of the bin he'd been reorganizing. As the immediate rush of not having gotten caught passed, the fear returned. He wasn't safe yet. Far from it. The truth had a way of worming to the surface. Luke knew Rick would eventually figure out what had happened and trace it back to him. Luke wished he'd stopped stealing long before. He wished he'd never started.

A new, even more worrisome thought came to him. He'd just been handed the perfect opportunity to tell Rick the truth, and he'd blown it. What if Rick *did* know? What if that little scene in the office had been a trick? What if it had been Rick's way of finding out just how dishonest Luke was? Maybe Rick was in his office at that very moment calling the police.

Luke's heart started to race, and he was tempted to run from the store. But then he spotted Rick behind the counter. He wasn't on the phone. He was talking to Adele—probably apologizing for having yelled at her. Luke calmed down and reminded himself that Rick wasn't exactly the devious type. If he suspected Luke, he'd come right out and say so.

Wouldn't he?

Eight

With great effort, Nikki had put her worries about Luke and Suzanne out of her mind. It wasn't easy not thinking about Suzanne when she was always around. Friday at lunch when Suzanne left the table to buy a soda, Nikki secretly invited Deb and Victoria to sleep over at her house. They both accepted, and Nikki was looking forward to spending some time alone with her two best friends, without Suzanne.

That afternoon Nikki rented videos and bought magazines and junk food. She was totally excited about spending some time with her old friends, friends she'd known since back when they'd had sleepovers for real—not just for a goof.

Nikki was tidying up her room when the phone rang. Fearing it might be Luke or Suzanne, she let the answering machine pick up.

"Hi, Nik?" came a voice after the beep. "It's Deb. I just—"

Nikki sprinted across the room and scooped up the phone. "Deb? Hi, I'm here."

"Oh, great!" Deb said. "I just wanted to let you know I'm running a little late. I just got home from the hospital."

Nikki sat down on her bed. "How's Katia?"

"She looked the same to me," Deb said. "But while I was there, I had a long talk with Mrs. Stein. She told me that the doctors say Katia's much better."

"Really?" Nikki could hardly believe what Deb was telling her. "That's fantastic!"

"I know," Deb said. "The doctors did some sort of test and found out the swelling in her brain has gone way down. That's supposed to be a good sign."

"Keith must be so psyched!" Nikki exclaimed. "What did he say?"

"He wasn't there," Deb said. "But I'm sure he's really happy. Hey, let's get off the phone so I can get over there. Should I bring anything?"

"Nope," Nikki said. "Everything's set."

"Okay, be right over," Deb said.

Nikki replaced the phone in its cradle. Her mood had improved quite a bit. She picked up the phone again and dialed Keith's number, wanting to share the good news with him personally. But Keith didn't pick up. As soon as his answering machine clicked on, Nikki put down the receiver. Keith's probably on his way to the hospital, she told herself.

Keith pulled his car into an empty space and parked. He jumped out without bothering to pull the emergency brake or pick up the CDs that covered the passenger seat.

As Keith crossed the parking lot he realized how different he felt. Lighter—as if he were walking on the moon.

Katia was improving! The doctors had told Keith's parents they were "hopeful." Hopeful! In the two weeks since Katia's accident, the doctors had carefully refrained from giving the Steins any reassurance whatsoever. If one of them said, "I think she looks better," the doctors had seemed to feel it was their duty to counter with, "There's been no change in her condition." Sometimes Keith had felt the medical staff were even afraid to smile in front of his family. But now—"hopeful!"

Keith felt like dancing. Like going out on the town. Like celebrating.

He felt lucky.

Keith opened the door and stepped into the building.

"Welcome to Pinewoods, sir," said a sexy blond woman standing beside the door.

Keith gave her a brilliant smile, but quickly moved on. He wasn't there to pick up girls; he was there to play cards. Since he had only five bucks in his pocket, that was going to take some doing. Luckily, Keith had friends in powerful places.

Sleazy Tony was at the bar, drinking with a guy who must have weighed about three hundred pounds. Keith sat on the red vinyl stool next to Tony's.

Tony turned around. "Hey, kid. What's happening?"

"I'm celebrating," Keith announced.

"Oh, yeah? Lemme guess. You just got your driver's license?"

"Very funny," Keith said. "No, I just got some great news. Listen, Tony, could you hook me up with a few bucks?"

The fat guy raised one eyebrow, and a smirk passed over his face. "What's the matter, Tony? Lowering your standards? Isn't this kid a bit green to take advantage of?"

"Am I taking advantage of you, Keith?"

"No."

"More like the other way around, right?" Tony asked, patting Keith on the back. "After all, you already owe me."

"I haven't forgotten about that," Keith said quickly.

"What did you do with the five C-notes I gave you last week?" Tony asked, his eyes fixed on Keith.

"I lost them," Keith admitted. "But I'll be able to pay you back real soon."

The fat guy popped a pretzel into his mouth. "Feeling lucky, kid?"

"Totally."

Tony pulled his wallet out of his cheap brown pants. The gesture reminded Keith of his father when he paid him his allowance. "How much do you need?"

Keith licked his lips. "How about a grand?" he asked as casually as he could.

Without a word, Tony peeled the bills off his wad.

Keith counted the money, folded it, and then slipped it into his own wallet. "Thanks," he said.

"You're welcome," Tony said politely. But as Keith turned to walk away, Tony grabbed his wrist. "Don't forget, kid, that's a loan. I expect it back."

Keith was shocked by Tony's sudden intensity. "Don't worry, man," he said nervously. "You'll get it back—every cent."

"Plus interest," the fat guy put in. "Don't forget the interest."

"Sure," Keith said. "Whatever."

Tony released Keith and smiled at him. "Have fun."

"Right," Keith said. He walked toward the poker tables, his nerves badly jangled. What was with Tony's tough-guy routine? He thought about marching right back to Tony and handing over his slimy money. Maybe he'd do that—after his first hand.

Keith firmly turned his back on a gorgeous female dealer and slid into a chair at a table with a male dealer. He didn't want any distractions. As soon as the cards were in his hands, Keith's confidence came back. So what if Tony was some kind of small-time hood? Keith was in charge. Tony had given him exactly what he wanted, hadn't he?

Keith's hand shook as he raised his glass of cola and took a sip.

His head reeled. He'd started off strong—gotten good cards, won a few hands. But less than an hour later, the thousand dollars he'd borrowed from Tony was neatly tucked in other people's wallets. Keith was flat broke. No, worse than that. He was fifteen hundred bucks in the hole.

Tony. Is he still around? Keith wondered as he put his half-finished soda down with a clunk. He had to get out of there before Tony saw him. Keith slipped off the bar stool, grabbed his jacket, and headed for the door.

Too late. Tony had just walked in, a toothpick clasped between his teeth. He greeted nearly everyone in the bar.

Keith stood rooted in the middle of the floor. He couldn't run away now. He fought down the panic that was threatening to overwhelm him.

Tony positioned himself at a table near the door. Spotting Keith, he casually motioned for him to approach.

Keith obeyed.

"What are you doing in here with the losers?" Tony asked, a big smile across his face. "I thought you came to play."

Tony's tone bucked up Keith's confidence. "I had a bad night," he said, shrugging one shoulder.

"A bad night?" Tony articulated each word. His smile was fading. "Is that your cute way of saying you've already lost all of my money?"

Keith's anger flashed. "Don't worry about your money. I'm gonna pay you back."

"Yeah? How?"

Good question. Where would Keith get fifteen hundred dollars? A few months before, he'd had a sizable chunk in the bank, but he'd blown all of that on a new stereo system for his car. He got a generous allowance, more than enough to buy gas and movie tickets, but it would take more than a year to save fifteen hundred bucks, forty dollars at a time.

Tony was glaring at Keith. He moved his toothpick to the other side of his mouth.

Keith was sure none of his friends could lend him that kind of money. His parents had it, but Keith couldn't ask them for it. No way. The idea of asking his parents was insane. Especially now. They had enough to worry about with Katia in the hospital.

Tony leaned closer. His face wasn't more than a foot away. "So, kid, come up with any bright ideas?"

Keith licked his lips. "There's only one way. You should lend me another grand."

"And what would you do with that?"

"Play poker."

"Only this time you'd win, right?"

"Right."

Tony fell back into his chair, exploding into laughter.

Keith allowed himself a spark of hope. He didn't like to be laughed at, but at least now Tony didn't look as if he was going to kill him any second. But then Tony's laughter died away. "That's the stupidest idea I've ever heard. You might not have realized it yet, but you don't have any particular talent for cards. Your loan application is denied."

Keith's fear was losing out to his anger. Who did this two-bit hood think he was, anyway? "Well, then, I don't have the faintest idea how I'm going to pay you back."

"Find a way."

"And if I don't?"

Tony smiled. "Then I'll just have to find something you can do for me."

Keith didn't like the sound of that. "Like what?"

"Get me the money, and you won't have to find out," Tony said. "Now get out of here. The sight of you makes me sick."

Keith hurried out of the bar area and across the casino floor. Fifteen hundred dollars. At first the words hadn't had any meaning to him. Now they sounded like a death sentence.

When Keith got home from the hospital on Sunday afternoon, the phone in his bedroom was ringing. It was his own private line, so nobody else would pick up. Keith took the stairs to the second floor two at a time. Dropping his backpack on his bed, he picked up the phone.

"Hello?"

"Keith?"

"Yeah? Who's this?"

"Tony. I need my money. Now."

Keith's blood ran cold. "How did you get my phone number?" It was unlisted.

"Don't you worry about that. I have my ways. Now how about my money?"

"I—I don't have it."

"Then get it."

"I'll need some time. . . ." Keith let his plea die away. Tony had already hung up.

Nine

"Have you guys read Sally's article?" Deb asked as she pulled a chair up to the lunch table.

Victoria rolled her eyes as she scooted over to give Deb more room. "Read it? People have been *quoting* it to me all day."

Hiding a smile, Deb glanced across the table at Nikki and Suzanne. Suzanne seemed to be concentrating on squeezing a packet of ketchup onto her french fries, but the sparkle in her eyes revealed her amusement. Nikki gave Deb a quick wink.

"Are you saying you didn't like it?" Deb asked Victoria innocently.

"No kidding, Sherlock. Of course I didn't like it!" Victoria exclaimed.

"Really? Why not?" Nikki asked, pretending to be surprised.

Deb ducked her head and started to unwrap

her lunch so that Victoria wouldn't see her smile. Nikki's clueless act wasn't convincing.

"Sally makes you guys look good," Victoria said. "But I come off like a witch. She makes it sound as if I'm always making obnoxious comments."

Actually, Sally had reported only two of the remarks Victoria had blurted out while Sally was hanging with their crowd. Deb actually thought Sally had gone easy on Victoria. She could have made her look much worse.

Victoria abruptly put down her can of diet soda. "You know, I wouldn't be surprised if what Sally did constitutes libel. Maybe I should get Mom to call our lawyer tonight. Do you think it's possible to sue a school newspaper?"

Suzanne started to giggle. Nikki was laughing, too, and Deb couldn't help joining in.

"What's so funny?" Victoria demanded.

"You," Suzanne said, pointing straight at Victoria.

"What about me?"

Nikki touched Victoria's arm. "I hate to break this to you, but you *are* obnoxious. Your lawsuit would be thrown out of court. Sally was right on the mark."

"How can you say that?" Victoria sounded wounded.

Nikki smiled and shook her head. "It's the truth. But don't worry, we love you anyway."

"If you got sweet on us, we'd go into shock,"

Suzanne added, popping a fry into her mouth.

"Ha, ha," Victoria sneered, eating a spoonful of strawberry yogurt.

Nikki shot Suzanne an impatient look.

As Deb took a bite of her ham sandwich, she decided something wasn't right between Nikki and Suzanne. She'd been surprised when Nikki hadn't invited Suzanne to her slumber party the weekend before. But whatever was going on, it was all beneath the surface. They still acted like the best of friends—most of the time.

"My English teacher spent the entire period today talking about Sally's articles," Deb reported.

"That's outrageous!" Victoria exclaimed. "What a waste of class time."

Coming from a girl who spent most of *her* class time writing notes to her friends and flirting, Deb found this a little hard to take. "Actually, it was the best class we had all year," she argued. "Mrs. Porter helped us see the subtext in Sally's articles."

"The *what?*" Victoria repeated.

"Subtext," Deb told her. "You know, the underlying message."

"And what was that?" Victoria demanded, taking another spoonful of her yogurt.

"That no group at school is really so different from the others," Deb said.

"Universality," Suzanne said. "English teachers love that."

141

"Well, I think it's nothing but a nauseatingly P.C., extra-crunchy load," Victoria commented. "Anyone who thinks I have something in common with those losers from the ramp needs to see a shrink."

Deb giggled. "Spoken like someone who never makes an obnoxious comment."

"Well, excuse me for having my own opinion," Victoria snapped back. "I don't care if everyone else goes around treating Sally like she just won the Pulitzer Prize. I'm not impressed. And I don't plan to take part in her little event, either."

"You mean the dress-as-someone-else day?" Suzanne asked.

"Whatever she's calling it," Victoria said, tossing her plastic spoon into the empty yogurt container.

That day's article had been the last in Sally's series. At the end she'd challenged everyone to leave their usual clothes at home the next day and dress like someone from a different crowd. Sally called it "getting into someone else's skin."

"I think it sounds like a blast," Deb said.

"I've always wanted to dress like a punk," Suzanne put in. "Maybe I'll dye my hair pink for the day."

"Do it!" Deb exclaimed.

"What about you, Nik?" Suzanne asked. "Are you going to wear something outrageous tomorrow?"

"I'm thinking about going grunge," Nikki announced, spearing a tomato with her fork. "But then again, I could put together a great—"

She stopped. Deb and the others waited. "You could put together a great what?" Deb prompted.

"I— Sorry." Nikki paused, playing with the salad in front of her. "I just saw Keith over by the lunch line. I was hoping he'd come over here, but he's heading the opposite way."

"So what's the big tragedy?" Victoria asked.

"I'm worried about him," Nikki said. "He was acting strange this morning. Distant. Like he was sleepwalking or something."

"We can't exactly expect him to act normal," Deb said. "He's under an awful lot of stress."

Suzanne nodded. "All those hours at the hospital, seeing his sister in a coma—it can't be easy."

"I guess that's what it is," Nikki said thoughtfully.

Suzanne and Deb went back to discussing what to wear on dress-as-someone-else day. Victoria went back to pretending to be uninterested.

Suzanne honestly didn't know what was wrong with her. How could she have forgotten something so important? She had a history paper due in exactly two days, and she hadn't even chosen a topic yet. Not just any paper, either, but one that counted for a quarter of her final grade. How could she have blanked out on something like that?

Actually, Suzanne had to admit, her lapse was hardly surprising. The last few weeks of her life had been crazy. She'd hardly had time to catch her breath, much less prepare an outline for a paper on a major figure in Colonial America.

Suzanne opened the glass door of the school library and stepped inside. She realized with a pang of guilt that she hadn't been in the large, sun-filled room since the first day of school, when her English class had gone on a tour.

She sat down at one of the big round library tables to skim her history textbook. Suzanne had hoped to write about a Colonial woman, but her book hardly even mentioned any. The only interesting one was Pocahontas, the Native American princess. Not exactly original—Suzanne was pretty sure she'd done a report on Pocahontas in the third grade.

Well, it was the best she could do at the last minute. Suzanne slammed her book shut and headed toward the computer. She did a search for books on Pocahontas. Only two titles scrolled up onto the screen. Great. Mr. Begley, her grouchy history teacher, had repeatedly told her class this paper wasn't a book report. They were required to use at least two sources. Suzanne printed out the book titles. If either of the books was checked out, she'd have to go downtown to the public library. What a drag.

Collecting her printout, Suzanne walked around the room, searching for the right call numbers. After wandering around in circles for at least five minutes, she hurried down an aisle—and almost crashed right into Luke.

"Whoa," he said. "Research isn't supposed to be a contact sport."

Suzanne felt her knees turn to water. She could see only one of Luke's startling blue eyes—the other was hidden behind a lock of his brown hair—but that was enough to send her pulse racing.

"What are you working on?" Luke asked.

"History report."

"Begley?"

"Begley."

Suzanne hated the fact that Luke had the same teacher she did, but a different period. Why couldn't he have been in her class? She tried to skim the spines of the books on the shelf, but she was having a hard time focusing on the call numbers. "I'm looking for a book on Pocahontas," she explained, her heart pounding with his closeness. "If someone's already checked it out, I'm dead meat."

"Is this it?" Luke asked, holding out a book with a mustard yellow binding.

"Yes! Luke, you're a lifesaver!"

"Actually, I can hardly swim."

Suzanne shook her head and smiled. Luke was totally hot—even when he was telling bad jokes. But her smile faded as an awful thought came into her head. "Wait, I can't take this book. You probably need it for your own report."

"It's okay," Luke assured her. "I can spare it. I've got about six other books at home."

"Still, you saw it first," Suzanne argued.

"Take it," Luke said, placing the book in her shaking hands. "I insist."

"Well, okay," Suzanne said slowly.

Luke was about to say something more, but then he seemed to remember something. He fell silent.

Suzanne had a good idea of what he'd remembered. No, not what, *who*. Nikki. She too had to keep reminding herself that Luke was Nikki's boyfriend. Her sister's boyfriend. But Suzanne was finding it harder and harder to worry about protecting Nikki's feelings. Perhaps that was because Nikki had been so cold to her lately. Suzanne had done everything she could to show her loyalty to Nikki. But Nikki seemed to resent it—or maybe resent *her*.

"Well, I—I'd better see if I can find the other book I need," Suzanne said awkwardly.

"Good luck," Luke told her.

"Thanks. And thanks again for this." Suzanne held up the history book.

"You're welcome."

Suzanne stole one more quick glance at Luke. She'd been forced to choose between Nikki and Luke, and she'd picked Nikki. Now she couldn't help wondering if she'd made the right choice.

Ten

"Hey, Nikki, looking good!" Sally called out as Nikki headed though the crowded hallways to the noisy lunchroom the next day.

"Thanks to you!" Nikki called back.

Hillcrest High was buzzing. Practically everyone had accepted Sally's challenge to dress differently for a day. People who looked like jocks were hanging out on the ramp, and the usually preppie crowd on the back steps was now sporting flannel, multicolored hair, and nose rings. The mixed-up scene had thrown everyone into a party mood.

As usual, Nikki was in the middle of everything. She was wearing holey jeans, a black T-shirt she'd bought at a Valhalla concert, a leather jacket, and much too much black eye makeup.

Fighting her way across the lunchroom, Nikki decided her outfit was one of the best.

147

"Hey, gorgeous," Luke greeted Nikki as she claimed the seat next to him at the table. They were the first to arrive. "I almost didn't recognize you."

Nikki had been annoyed at Luke ever since he'd defended Suzanne at the Tunesmith. Now she felt an added twinge of aggravation. Luke was dressed in his usual clothes: white T-shirt, black jeans, and his favorite old gas-station jacket.

"What's wrong with you?" she demanded. "You knew today was dress-as-someone-else day. Why can't you get into the spirit of things for once?"

Luke shrugged. "I wasn't trying to make a statement or anything. Sally's idea is cool. It's just that I don't think of myself as belonging to any one group. I'm just me. I didn't have any idea of what to wear."

Nikki's irritation grew. Luke sounded as if he placed himself above them all. *They* could be pigeonholed, but *he* was unique. Talk about a major ego.

"Hi, you guys!" Suzanne pulled up a chair on the other side of the table. "Hasn't today been great?"

"Yeah," Luke agreed. "It's made me look at everyone a whole new way. I never realized clothes were so important."

Nikki was stung. A minute ago, Luke had put down dress-as-someone-else day. But now that

Suzanne had expressed enthusiasm, he was acting as if it were some kind of brilliant experiment. Why did everyone in Nikki's life find Suzanne so endlessly charming?

And that wasn't the only thing. Suzanne also had chosen to dress as a smoker that day, and Nikki had to admit Suzanne's outfit blew hers away. Suzanne was wearing holey jeans similar to Nikki's. But she also had on an incredibly cool pair of black biker boots and a beat-up Harley-Davidson T-shirt. She was wearing silver rings on eight of her fingers. One was shaped like a peace sign, another like a snake.

Suzanne turned to Nikki. "I love your outfit," she said.

"Thanks," Nikki said, plastering on her best fake smile. Inside, she had given up pretending to like Suzanne. Her friendly feelings had been completely overtaken by jealousy and resentment.

Keith walked toward them. His dress-as-someone-else outfit was lame. He'd thrown a flannel shirt over his usual polo shirt and traded his everyday running shoes for a pair of work boots. But at least he made an effort, Nikki thought. Unlike some people.

"Hi," Keith grunted as he turned a chair around backward and sat down in it, next to Nikki.

"Hi," Nikki said.

She was glad to see Keith. Ever since the day

before, she'd been unable to shake the feeling that something was very wrong with him. Keith's other friends assumed he was upset about Katia, but Nikki didn't think that was it. After all, Katia's condition was improving.

"How are things going?" Nikki asked Keith gently.

He shrugged one shoulder. "Okay, I guess."

Nikki watched as Keith ate his sandwich in silence. He was hardly looking at his friends. Nikki glanced at Luke and Suzanne. They were busy talking to a girl Nikki recognized but didn't know, and weren't paying any attention to Keith. They all must have had the same history teacher, because they were discussing some hideous paper he'd assigned them.

"Hey, uh . . . Nikki," Keith said awkwardly. "Could you lend me some money?"

"Sure," Nikki said automatically. She reached for her book bag and pulled out her wallet. Assuming Keith needed the money for a soda, she handed him a dollar.

Keith just stared at the money.

"What's the matter?" Nikki asked.

Keith licked his lips. "Actually, I was hoping to borrow a little more."

"Oh." Nikki flipped through the bills in her wallet, then pulled them all out. "All I've got is twelve bucks. Here, take it." She pressed the money into Keith's hand.

Keith smoothed it out, a strange smile

playing over his features. "You know what? Never mind. I don't need it after all."

Keith pushed the money toward Nikki, stood up, and crumpled his lunch bag into a ball. "Later," he said, addressing the whole table.

Nikki watched him walk through the chaotic lunchroom. Something was definitely not right with him, and she was almost positive it had nothing to do with Katia.

"That's it for today," Coach Kostro snarled late on Tuesday afternoon. "But I'm warning you lazy, good-for-nothing mama's boys—another practice like that, and I'm going to get mad!"

Keith was too exhausted to talk as he trooped back to the locker room with the other players. Every muscle in his body ached. Since Katia's accident, Keith had been able to attend practices only a few days a week. All of that down time was affecting his speed. He knew he wasn't in top condition.

Practice that afternoon had been brutal. Keith had had a hard time connecting with the ball. And even when he did manage to catch it, he'd never completed a down. Some defensive player always tackled him before he'd taken more than a few steps forward.

Keith wished he could have blamed his miserable performance on his physical condition. That was something he could change. But he knew his problems were mental.

"Hey, Stein," Pete Brewer called out as the boys crowded into the locker room. *"Excellent* practice today."

Ignoring him, Keith peeled off his filthy practice uniform.

"Yeah, my *grandma* could have tackled you," Chris Bauer, a bruiser of a fullback, put in.

The rest of the team exploded into laughter.

"Hey, you twerps," John barked out. "Chill out!"

The room was silent for a moment, then the other guys started to whisper. Keith didn't have to listen to know what they were murmuring about: Katia's coma, the strain Keith was under, what an idiot Chris had been. Funny thing was, they didn't know the half of it.

As Keith walked by, a sheepish-looking Chris put out a hand. "Hey, man, I'm sorry. I didn't mean anything by it."

"Forget it," Keith said, stepping around Chris and heading straight for the showers.

Turning the hot water on full, Keith let the warm spray ease his aches and pains. But even the steamy water didn't relax him.

Keith had been jumpy ever since Tony's phone call two days earlier. In his head, he'd replayed their short conversation hundreds of times, analyzing every word.

Only one thing about it was comforting: Tony hadn't actually threatened him. But his voice hadn't been friendly, either. Keith had no doubt

Tony planned to get his fifteen hundred bucks, whatever it took.

Keith hadn't slept well the past two nights. He'd tossed and turned and tried to think of a way out of this mess. But none of his options looked good. Nobody he knew would be willing to part with that much money, except his parents. And they'd demand an explanation in return—an explanation Keith wasn't willing to provide.

"Hey, Stein, you okay?" John called. "You've been in there forever."

"Feels good," Keith grunted in reply.

"Whatever turns you on, man," John said. "I'm heading over to the hospital. See you there."

"Yeah, later," Keith replied, keeping his eyes closed.

By the time Keith finally dragged himself out of the shower, most of the other players had gone. He dried off and dressed slowly.

Keith was heading across the nearly deserted parking lot toward his car when he spotted Tony. He was leaning up against a big black Lincoln Continental parked right in front of the school. When Tony saw Keith, he knocked on one of the car's tinted windows. A huge, powerful-looking man dressed in a cheap pinstriped suit emerged from the car.

"Hey, kid," Tony called. He was chewing on a toothpick. "I want to talk to you."

153

Keith's first instinct was to run. He could make a break for his car. He wouldn't have any trouble outrunning Tony and his muscle-bound friend. But what was the point? Obviously Tony had no trouble tracking Keith down. Running would probably only make him angrier. *I need to talk some sense into this creep*, Keith reasoned. *I can't pay him money I don't have.*

Tony waited as Keith approached, never moving from his leaning position. "Have you got my three grand?" Tony asked when Keith was close enough so that he didn't have to yell.

"Three grand?" It came out a squeak. Keith's mouth had gone dry.

"That's right, three grand."

"You must have made some kind of mistake." Keith kept his eyes on Tony's face. "I only owe you fifteen hundred."

"No, fifteen hundred is what you *owed* me Saturday," Tony said. "Since then, some interest has accrued."

"A hundred percent? That's ridiculous!"

Tony took a step closer, his face only inches from Keith's own. Keith could smell his sour breath. "For a bank it's ridiculous. But, as you may have noticed, I ain't no bank."

"Well, I don't have it," Keith said, turning his jeans pockets inside out. "I'm very sorry, but I don't have fifteen hundred bucks, much less three grand."

Tony considered Keith for a long moment.

Behind him, the huge guy shifted impatiently.

"What can I do?" Keith asked, his nervousness creeping into his voice.

"Well, as I see it, you have two choices." Tony jerked a thumb in the direction of the monster behind him. "Option one: My little friend here can do some disrespect to your legs. Say, break each one of them in three places—one for each grand you owe me."

Keith felt sick. Tony was probably bluffing, but he couldn't be sure. "What's my other option?"

Tony smiled slightly. "Wise man. I thought you might be interested in that. Well, option two is a little less violent. We get to stay friends, and you agree to repay a favor with a favor. Friendly-like."

Keith didn't see anything even remotely friendly about Tony and his overfed sidekick, but he was stuck. "What do you have in mind?" Keith asked, keeping a wary eye on Tony's not-so-friendly giant.

The bookie broke into an oily grin. "Why don't you get into the car? I have an idea of just how you might be useful to me."

The Neanderthal opened one of the car's back doors and motioned for Keith to get in.

Keith hesitated. "You want to talk now?"

"No time like the present, kid."

Keith looked from Tony to the goon, then back again. While he was hesitating, the big guy

155

put his hand on Keith's back and shoved him inside the car. They're going to kill me, Keith thought, his heart thudding in his chest. And there's nothing I can do to stop them.

Luke was in no hurry to get to the Tunesmith that afternoon. Actually, he was dreading it. Rick was holding the first-ever Tunesmith employee meeting. Every employee was required to be there, and the store was closed for the event. It didn't take a lot of imagination to guess what Rick wanted to talk to them about.

Finally Luke had no choice but to go in or miss the meeting. Inside he found Adele, Mark, and all the other employees crowded into Rick's little office. Rick was sitting behind his desk, not talking to anyone, and looking totally uncomfortable.

The employees were sitting on all the available chairs or on the floor, or were leaning up against the walls. Some of them looked worried, others confused. Some just seemed irritated by the whole thing.

As Luke slipped in the door and went to sit next to Mark, Rick glanced at his watch. "Okay, I think everyone's here," he said. "I know we've all got better things to do today, so let's get started."

There were grumbles of approval.

"I'm going to get right to the point," Rick said. "After doing the inventory this month, it's become clear that one or more of you has been taking money out of the register."

"What?" Mark exclaimed.

Adele let out a low whistle.

The room grew noisy as the employees discussed this surprising piece of information.

Rick put his hand up for quiet. "I don't blame you for being disturbed. This has been keeping me up nights. Let me assure you that this is no idle accusation. I've looked into and eliminated every other possibility. I never would have brought this up unless I was absolutely sure."

The employees all looked very nervous now, as if each one was expecting Rick to accuse him or her. Luke was sick with guilt. If it hadn't been for him, none of them would have had to endure this awkward scene.

"I don't have to tell you this is a serious situation," Rick continued. "I'm going to give the guilty party one week to step forward. If he or she doesn't, I'm going to fire *all* of you."

The room erupted with the employees' angry comments.

"No way!"

"That's not fair!"

Again Rick held up his hand. "This is the only way." He stood quietly for a moment, studying their faces. "Okay, that's it," he announced. "Everyone can go."

The employees marched out of Rick's office.

"This really stinks," Mark commented. "I

can't believe I'm going to lose my job because of some idiot who can't keep his hands out of the register."

Adele was more hopeful. "Don't freak out yet," she said with a shrug. "Maybe the thief will step forward."

"Fat chance," Mark groused.

"Come on, Mark," Adele urged. "Think positively!" But Adele's optimism wasn't contagious. Mark still had a glum expression as he walked out of the store. Luke knew better than anyone that Mark was right. They would all be out of work next week. Luke had to keep his stealing a secret. If he told Rick the truth, he'd never get another job in Hillcrest, and he couldn't afford to let that happen. Even if everyone else had to suffer, too.

Deb paused outside the closed door to Katia's hospital room. "I keep thinking I should knock," she said as she pushed against the door and held it open so Nikki, Victoria, and Suzanne could follow her inside.

"I know what you mean," Nikki said. "I can just imagine Katia calling out for us to come in."

"Look at these flowers!" Suzanne exclaimed, gazing at a gorgeous bouquet of ruby red roses on a table near the door. "I bet they're from John."

While the others were admiring the flowers, Deb sat in the chair right next to Katia's bed.

Glancing back at her friends, she took a deep breath. "Hi, Katia. The gang's all here. . . ." Her voice trailed off.

"Deb?" Suzanne asked. "Is something wrong?"

"No," Deb said in an excited whisper. "I—I think she actually looks better."

The other girls came closer.

"What do you mean, better?" Victoria asked suspiciously.

"I'm not sure," Deb admitted. "She just looks different to me."

"You're right," Suzanne decided, leaning over to get a closer look.

Nikki nodded eagerly. "Her skin tone is better, I think."

The mood in the room picked up. For the next half hour, the four girls chatted with each other and told Katia what had been happening in their lives. They didn't leave until an exhausted-looking Mrs. Stein arrived, asking for some time alone with her daughter.

"I think she's going to make it," Deb said out in the corridor.

"Well, don't get your hopes up too high," Victoria said.

Deb found Victoria's relentless pessimism irritating. She turned to Nikki and Suzanne. "Is anybody into grabbing a snack? I'm starved."

"No, thanks," Nikki said right away. "I've got to get home."

"Suzanne?"

"Sure. Let's go to the Organic Grape," Suzanne suggested.

"Sounds good," Deb agreed. "You coming, Victoria?"

"No, thanks," she said briskly.

Nikki and Victoria headed off toward the parking lot, and Deb and Suzanne walked the short distance downtown. Suzanne hardly spoke on the way there. She seemed preoccupied.

At the small restaurant, Deb and Suzanne put their books down on a corner table to save it and went to the counter together. Suzanne ordered a fresh juice shake, and Deb decided on a tofu taco. They paid, and carried their trays back to their little table by the window.

Suzanne looked thoughtful as she unwrapped her straw. "Deb—has Nikki said anything to you about me?"

"What do you mean?" Deb asked.

Suzanne cleared her throat. "Listen, you don't have to answer if you don't want to, but I was just wondering if Nikki told you why she's mad at me—if she *is* mad at me, that is. I mean, I don't even know for sure that she's mad, but she's been acting kind of weird—friendly one minute, distant the next."

Deb broke a piece of whole-wheat tortilla off her taco and chewed it as she considered how to answer. Nikki *had* been acting strange lately. And then there was that slumber party Suzanne hadn't been invited to. Deb was pretty sure

Suzanne didn't even know anything about it.

"She hasn't said anything to me," Deb said truthfully.

"Maybe I'm just paranoid," Suzanne said.

"No," Deb said. "Nikki really has been acting kind of odd recently. But it probably has nothing to do with you. Try not to worry about it."

Suzanne gave her a wry smile. "All right. Let's talk about something else."

"Okay," Deb said. "Tell me what you decided to do about your father."

"My father?" Suzanne's voice squeaked.

"I was just wondering if you've decided to look for him," Deb said. "But if you don't feel like talking about it. . . ."

Suzanne was looking down at the table. "I don't mind. It's just that I—I haven't been thinking much about it."

"Really?" Deb asked in surprise. "I've hardly been thinking about anything else. I try to forget about the fact that I'm adopted, but I can't make myself."

"Why try?" Suzanne asked. "If it's so important to you, I think you should go for it."

"You do?"

"Absolutely."

"You know, in my dreams, my birth parents are always happy to see me," Deb said. "But when I really think about it, I realize it probably won't be that way. After all, they made the decision to give me away. They might not be thrilled to have me drop back into their lives."

"I guess you have to make a decision. Can you live without knowing who your birth parents are? Or are you dying to meet them? If you really want to know them, it's probably worth the risk."

"I'm more worried about hurting other people," Deb said. "My real parents, the ones who raised me. My brother. My birth parents. There are so many people to consider."

By the time the girls left the Organic Grape an hour later, they had discussed all of the problems Deb might stumble across if she decided to search for her birth parents.

It wasn't until later, when Deb was up in her room starting her homework, that she realized they'd never discussed how Suzanne felt about her own missing father. And they'd completely dropped the topic of Nikki's odd behavior. At first Deb felt a bit guilty. Then she remembered how Suzanne had steered their conversation away from the topic of her father. Why didn't Suzanne want to talk about her father? Why was she being so secretive?

Eleven

I've got to calm down, Suzanne told herself sternly on Wednesday afternoon. She was standing in the hallway outside the school auditorium. Auditions for *West Side Story* were already well underway. Mr. Cadenza had encouraged all of the kids who were trying out to invite their friends, and the auditorium was far from empty.

Suzanne knew Mr. Cadenza wanted to create the experience of performing in front of a crowd so he could see how poised they would be up on the big stage. Suzanne had to admit it was a good strategy. Without an audience there, her nerves would never have been stretched so tight.

Suzanne knew her song backward and forward. She'd perfected every note, every rhythm. But she was *still* unsatisfied with the way she performed it. As much as she had practiced, the song always seemed flat. It lacked a spark.

The backstage door opened, and Nikki tiptoed out into the hallway. She'd been watching the auditions from the side of the stage.

"What's going on out there?" Suzanne asked quietly.

"Melissa Pressman is singing," Nikki reported. "I had to get out of there. I was feeling sick."

Suzanne's own stomach lurched. "Is she doing a good job?"

"Of course," Nikki said, rolling her eyes. "Her range is incredible. She can hit notes I can't even approach."

"I know," Suzanne said. "But remember, that's not the only thing Mr. Cadenza's looking for. You have much more stage presence than Melissa. She always gets nervous and taps her foot."

Nikki smiled thinly. "Thanks, but I'm so nervous I'm probably going to develop a tic, too."

The sound of applause drifted back into the hallway.

Suzanne took a deep breath, threw her shoulders back, and summoned a smile onto her face. "We'd better go in," she said. "I'm up next."

"I'll watch from the wings," Nikki told her. "Just glance over if you need moral support. I'll be right there."

Suzanne gave Nikki a grateful grin. She was

glad her friend was on her side that afternoon. One of Nikki's weird sulky moods would have undermined Suzanne's confidence even further.

Mr. Cadenza called her name, and Suzanne stepped out onto the stage. She handed the pianist her music and whispered a few instructions to him. Then she placed one hand on the piano and stood up a little straighter. As the pianist shuffled through the sheet music to familiarize himself with the piece she'd chosen, Suzanne scanned the auditorium. Mr. Cadenza was sitting in the second row. Another music teacher and one of the English teachers were sitting with him. Mr. Cadenza must have asked them to help judge the auditions. They were all holding clipboards and looked incredibly official.

Suzanne's eye strayed to the back of the auditorium, where she spotted Deb, Victoria, Keith—and Luke. At the sight of Luke's handsome face, a smile spread across her own face. She had to remind herself Luke was there for Nikki, not her.

"Ready when you are," the pianist announced.

Suzanne nodded slowly. The pianist began to play. Suzanne started to sing "Someday," the lush, romantic ballad she'd chosen—and, as always, she felt as if it sounded lifeless. But then her nervous gaze fell again on Luke. He was leaning forward in his seat, smiling his encouragement.

Thinking about Luke, Suzanne realized the lyrics she was singing were more than the ramblings of a sentimental songwriter. They could have been written about her relationship with Luke.

> *Your eyes tell a story*
> *Your lips will not say.*

> *But my eyes keep watching,*
> *Waiting, all day.*

Suzanne continued to gaze at Luke. His eyes never wavered from her face. She sang every line directly to him.

> *You'll come to me someday*
> *And you won't have to explain.*

> *For your eyes tell a story*
> *And my heart hears it plain.*

Suzanne imagined that Luke somehow knew she meant the words she was singing, and knew she was singing them to him. She wanted him to know how she felt, yet she could never just come out and tell him how much she loved him.

As Suzanne finished singing, the group in the auditorium applauded enthusiastically. She bit back a smile. She'd nailed the song.

Trying not to show her excitement, Suzanne

took a casual bow and collected her music from the pianist. Then she skipped down the stairs at the front of the stage and hurried up the aisle to join her friends before Nikki started singing.

"You were great," Luke whispered as she slid into the seat next to him.

Deb smiled and eagerly nodded. "That was beautiful."

"Thanks!" Suzanne sat back with a happy sigh. After weeks of preparation, she was relieved the audition was finally over. And, of course, she was happy she had sung so well. She hoped Nikki would do well, too.

Nikki took a deep breath and nodded at the pianist. As he played the introduction to her song, Nikki's eyes traveled over the people gathered in the auditorium. There was Mr. Cadenza with his clipboard, an encouraging smile lighting up his face.

Where's Luke? Nikki wondered. He promised to be here. Just as the pianist finished the introduction, Nikki spotted him sitting way in the back. He was leaning over to whisper something to the person sitting next to him—Suzanne!

Nikki tried to concentrate on hitting the first note of her song, which was high and difficult. But she couldn't stop staring at Suzanne, who was grinning like the Cheshire Cat.

"One and two and . . . ," the pianist whispered.

A counting pianist could mean only one

thing—she had fallen behind the beat. Nikki closed her eyes and tried to concentrate. A difficult quick passage was coming up. She would never get all the notes right unless she gave them her undivided attention. But as Nikki sang, a flood of images came rushing into her mind. Suzanne with her arms around Luke. Suzanne laughing at one of her father's jokes. Suzanne and Deb whispering together.

Suzanne jumping into the rushing river . . . swimming toward Nikki . . . coming to save her life.

That was the one image that had made Nikki forgive Suzanne for all the others.

But hadn't Nikki done enough to repay Suzanne? She'd accepted her as a friend, made her a part of the gang, thrown her a party. Was Nikki also expected to hand over her friends, her father, and her boyfriend?

The pianist was picking out certain notes, subtly emphasizing the melody of her song. Nikki realized she must have wandered off-key.

She tried to correct her rhythm and her pitch, but she could hardly breathe. Tears were gathering in her throat. Her eyes shifted to Mr. Cadenza. His face was unreadable. Luke was watching her intently. Suzanne had a worried frown as she leaned over to whisper something to him.

The tears were choking her now, and Nikki let her voice trail off. The pianist continued to play, shooting Nikki an anxious look. For a long moment Nikki stared out into the audience, mesmerized by the sight of Suzanne surrounded by her friends. Then she stormed offstage. She knew she was making a scene, but she didn't care.

Nikki didn't stop until she reached the hallway behind the auditorium. She leaned up against the cold cement-block wall and let the tears come.

Melissa Pressman tiptoed into the hallway. "Are you okay?" she asked tentatively.

Nikki turned her face toward the wall. "Please, just leave me alone!" Twisting away from Melissa, Nikki stumbled toward the exit. She had to get out of there. She had to put space between herself and all the people who'd just witnessed her complete humiliation.

Halfway down the hall, Nikki stopped. Suzanne was heading toward her.

"Nikki? What happened? Are you all right?" Suzanne rushed to her side.

The concern in her voice made Nikki wince. She'd had enough of Suzanne's I'm-your-best-friend routine.

"What happened out there?" Suzanne continued. "It seemed like you forgot the song—which is impossible, since we practiced it together a few thousand times."

Nikki tried to push past Suzanne, but Suzanne put out a hand to stop her. "Don't be upset," she said. "There will be other auditions. Everyone knows you have a beautiful voice. You just had an off day."

Suzanne's act is exceptional, Nikki told herself. Anyone watching us would believe Suzanne really cares about me. But Nikki couldn't shut out the thought that her off day was going to create some nice benefits for Suzanne. She'd probably get to play Maria now. As a fresh flood of tears overcame her, Nikki wondered what else Suzanne would steal from her.

After taking a deep breath, Nikki looked squarely into Suzanne's face. "Why don't you drop the innocent act?" she demanded.

"What?"

"*What?*" Nikki mimicked. "You know very well what I'm talking about. You call yourself my friend, but that's nothing but a big joke. You don't want to be my friend—you want to *steal* my friends."

"That's not true," Suzanne said quietly. She glanced at something behind Nikki's back, and Nikki turned to see that Melissa was still standing there, watching them.

Nikki turned angrily back to Suzanne. She didn't care who heard them arguing. "It's true, and you know it," she said, her voice rising. "But I'm through standing by and letting it happen. Go get your own life. Get your own boyfriend, and get your own father!"

Nikki saw the hurt in Suzanne's eyes, and she

treasured it. This time when she tried to push by Suzanne, Suzanne didn't resist.

Nikki rushed out of the building, elated. Her true feelings were out, and it was an immense relief. She and Suzanne were officially at war, and Nikki was ready for battle.

Suzanne leaned against the wall and watched Nikki race away from her. Melissa was still standing at the end of the hall, seemingly unsure of what to do next. Suzanne was too shocked and hurt to cry.

Ever since she and Nikki had made up after she'd kissed Luke, and especially since she'd discovered Nikki was her sister, Suzanne had made endless sacrifices for her. She'd tried to ignore Luke. She'd put up with Victoria. She'd been understanding about Nikki's strange moodiness. Nothing had been more important to her than Nikki's friendship.

Now, all of a sudden, Nikki had turned on her for no reason at all. Suzanne knew this wasn't just about the auditions. Something much deeper than that was bothering Nikki.

Suzanne didn't know what to think, except that Nikki would behave differently if she knew the truth about them. . . .

"Mr. and Mrs. Stein?" a doctor with a long blond ponytail asked politely. "May I have a word with you in private, please?"

171

"Sure," Mr. Stein said, getting to his feet.

As she and her husband walked toward the door, Mrs. Stein rested a hand briefly on Victoria's shoulder. "We'll be right back."

Victoria smiled at her.

After the door had silently closed behind the adults, Victoria shifted in her seat. John was sitting across the room from her. They'd been taking turns reading *The Scarlet Letter*, a book they were studying in their English class, to Katia.

John glanced up and flashed Victoria a grin. He placed the open book face down on his lap. "Let's take a break."

"Good idea," she said. "Hey, are you psyched about the opening game? I can't believe it's next week."

"Psyched?" John repeated as he rolled his head from side to side. "Worried is more like it. I've missed so many practices I've lost count."

Victoria slipped out of her seat and went to stand behind John. She placed her hands on his shoulders and began rubbing the knotted muscles in his neck. John's muscles were so *amazing*.

"Well, don't worry," Victoria said softly as her hands continued to work. "Walnut Hills always has a lame team. Remember last year? We totally crushed them."

"Yeah, it's lucky we drew them for the season opener. I could sleep through the entire game, and we'd still pound them. Mmm, that feels good."

"You're really tense," Victoria commented, enjoying the massage as much as John seemed to be.

John leaned his head back and smiled at her. "Not for long. Thanks to you."

"I could think of a better way. . . ." As Victoria was speaking a movement caught her eye. "What—"

In a flash John jumped out of his chair. He knelt next to Katia's bed. "Did you see that?" he demanded.

"I saw something," Victoria said. "What was it?"

"Katia! Her hand moved. I'm sure of it." Gently John took Katia's hand in his. "Kat, can you hear me? It's John. I'm right here with you."

For the next several seconds Victoria hardly dared to breathe. Maybe, just maybe, the moment she'd been dreading for weeks was about to arrive. . . .

No sound came from Katia.

John turned to Victoria. "You saw it, too, didn't you?" he asked desperately.

Victoria nodded.

"Go get a doctor," John ordered her as he turned back to Katia.

Victoria raced out into the hallway. Hurrying toward the nurses' station, she tried to calm herself. But she couldn't shake her panic or slow her racing mind. *What if Katia comes to? What if she identifies Dad's car?*

If that happens, my life is over, she thought grimly.

Victoria spotted Mr. and Mrs. Stein sitting in the waiting area, still talking to the ponytailed doctor.

"What's wrong?" Mrs. Stein asked as Victoria ran up to them.

"It's Katia!"

"What about Katia?" Mr. Stein grabbed Victoria's arm.

"We—John and I—we think we saw her move!"

The adults jumped to their feet and ran down the hall. Victoria hesitated, then hurried after them. Whatever happened, she wanted to know about it. She couldn't take any more suspense.

As the group burst into Katia's room John turned to them eagerly.

"It's definite," he announced. "She squeezed my hand a second ago. And I saw her eyelids flutter."

Mrs. Stein ran around to the far side of the bed. Mr. Stein stood behind his wife. They both watched Katia intently. The doctor, at the end of the bed, seemed less frantic but also deeply interested.

"Katia, darling, it's me, Mommy," Mrs. Stein whispered.

Victoria crept up until she was standing just behind John.

"Can you hear me, sweetie?" Mrs. Stein

continued, her voice choked with unshed tears.

Slowly, but naturally, as if she hadn't just spent weeks without moving, Katia turned her head toward her mother's voice. Victoria barely had time to gasp before Katia opened her eyes.

"Where am I?" Katia's voice was husky, but she sounded like herself.

"In the hospital," Mrs. Stein told her, tears running down her face.

"In the hospital?" Katia repeated. Her eyes flicked around the room. "Why?"

Victoria's hopes soared. *It's going to be okay! She doesn't even know where she is!*

"You were in a car accident," her mother whispered.

Katia licked her lips. "I remember now," she rasped out. "We were at Nikki's party. Victoria offered to drive me home." With that, Katia turned to smile at Victoria, apparently pleased to see her standing there.

Victoria smiled back, but she felt as if her heart were in a vise. *Katia remembers . . . but how much?*

A puzzled look crossed Katia's face. "I remember being in Victoria's car. It was raining. But I can't remember what happened next. . . ."

John squeezed Katia's hand, and she turned to face him. "Someone ran the car off the road."

Katia turned her eyes back to Victoria. "Are you okay?" she asked.

175

Victoria nodded, not trusting herself to speak.

"What about the people in the other car?" Katia asked. "Was anyone hurt?"

"No, precious," Mrs. Stein told her. "They just drove away."

"Well, I hope they weren't hurt," Katia said faintly.

Immense relief flooded through Victoria. She didn't see the car! She doesn't know Dad hit us!

Katia closed her eyes.

"Katia?" John whispered urgently.

"What's the matter?" Mr. Stein demanded.

"Don't worry," the doctor said, her eyes on the monitors. "She's only sleeping. I'll call the specialists in and they can check her more thoroughly, but I feel confident enough to say you have reason to celebrate. It looks like Katia is going to be fine."

Victoria had been clenching her hands into fists so tight, her fingernails had dug red crescents into her palms. Now she allowed herself to relax. Katia hadn't seen a thing!

Mrs. Stein grabbed her husband's arm, her eyes brimming with tears. "I can hardly believe it!"

Mr. Stein gave his wife a tight hug. "She's going to be all right," he murmured into her hair. "Our baby is going to be all right."

Mrs. Stein pulled back. "We've got to call Keith!" She hurried over to the bedside table and started to punch in the phone number.

"Don't forget to call your mother," Mr. Stein said.

Mrs. Stein looked up with an ecstatic smile. "I'm going to call everybody I've ever met!"

John hadn't left Katia's side. He bent over and tenderly kissed her cheek. "Sweet dreams," he whispered.

Victoria's blood ran cold. Sweet dreams? She could hardly believe John had uttered those words. Where had this sensitivity come from all of a sudden? He'd certainly never shown it toward *her*. Maybe she'd been too quick to decide that Katia's recovery was harmless. . . .

Victoria reached out and grabbed John's shoulder. "Let's go," she whispered harshly. "The Steins should be alone."

"You're right," John whispered back. But several seconds passed before he dragged his eyes away from Katia's face.

"We'll see you tomorrow," Victoria told the Steins briskly.

"Fine, fine," Mr. Stein said absently.

Mrs. Stein was talking on the phone; she gave Victoria a quick nod and smile.

Victoria tapped her foot while she waited for John to gather his belongings and say his goodbyes. When his eyes drifted back toward Katia, Victoria's patience ran out.

"I'll wait for you outside," she snapped at John. She paced back and forth in front of

Katia's room for several minutes before he burst out into the hallway.

"Wasn't that incredible?" John asked as he joined Victoria. "I can't believe she woke up just like that!"

"Incredible," Victoria said in a flat tone. She slipped an arm through John's as they started toward the elevators. "So, want to grab a cup of coffee—or go see a movie?"

"I just wish she'd stayed awake longer," John said. "There's so much I want to tell her!"

"Like what?" Victoria demanded.

"Like I was happy to hear her voice."

"You were *happy to hear her voice?*" Victoria repeated in a mocking tone. She took a step away from John. "You're unreal!"

"What?"

"I guess you're pretty happy right about now, huh?"

John looked baffled. "Sure. Why? Aren't *you* happy about Katia?"

"I would be if you weren't acting like a lovesick idiot!" Victoria snapped.

"She *is* my girlfriend," John said, his voice sharp.

Victoria's eyebrows flew up. "Then what am I?"

A passing nurse gave them a disapproving frown. Victoria was too angry to care, but John grabbed her arm and led her into a nearby waiting room.

"Listen," he said in a low, calm voice. "I don't

want to fight with you. I mean, you're the best friend I have. I couldn't have gotten through the past few weeks without you."

"And now that Katia's better, you're going to dump me!"

"What do you mean, *dump* you?" John asked. "We were never going out."

"No, we were just *making* out!"

John smiled, but when Victoria continued to glare at him, his expression grew serious.

"I understand how you might have gotten the wrong idea," he said carefully. "But I didn't think you were still interested in me . . . *that* way."

Tears sprang up in Victoria's eyes. She lowered her head, hiding her face behind a veil of hair so John wouldn't see her cry.

"I love Katia," John continued softly. "I care about you, too—but in a different way."

Victoria felt a surge of anger, and she shook her hair out of her face. "Fine," she said furiously. "Don't let me take up any more of your time. You have terrific news to spread. Your precious Katia is back among the living."

"Don't be mad," John pleaded.

With a sudden movement Victoria reached out and smacked him across the face. "Don't tell me what to feel!"

After one satisfying look at John's stunned expression, Victoria stormed down the hall. She flung open the door to the staircase and started down the steps.

John thinks I'm his friend? What a joke! Friends don't use each other.

John's betrayal added to the hurt Victoria already felt over being ignored by Ian Houghton. She was fed up with Hillcrest High boys. *I'm never dating another high-school guy again,* she promised herself. *I don't care if I have to live like a nun for the rest of the year. College—and college men—can't come soon enough.*

After practice on Thursday afternoon, Keith sank down on a bench in the locker room. The rest of the football team crowded all around him. As they got ready to hit the showers, the noise level rose. The big season opener was that weekend, and the entire team was on a natural high. The long weeks of training were finally over. That weekend the glory would begin.

"Nice work today, Dover," John called out.

"Thanks, man," Michael Dover, a stocky receiver, replied. "It was great having you out there this afternoon. We really missed you the last few weeks."

"Believe me, I'm glad to be back."

"Yeah, the news about Katia is awesome," Michael said. "She's a sweet kid."

"The best," John agreed.

There was a pause, and Keith glanced up. John and Michael were watching him, and he realized they expected him to say something about his sister's amazing recovery. All he could manage was a weak smile.

Even after Michael headed off to the shower, Keith was aware that John was watching him. John put one foot up on the bench and started to untie his cleats. Keith stared at the muddy shoe, feeling half dead.

"You going to shower?" John asked him.

Keith pushed himself to his feet. "Yeah, I guess so."

"What's up with you?" John asked. "You should be on top of the world. Katia's going to be okay!"

"I know. Listen, I've got to talk to you."

"So talk."

Keith glanced around the locker room. A few of the other guys had grabbed their stuff and gone, but the showers were full. Plenty of people were still around.

"Privately," Keith said.

John raised his eyebrows but seemed amused by Keith's request. "Whatever."

"Meet me at my car," Keith suggested. "I'll drive you home."

"I've got my car here."

"Fine," Keith said, irritation creeping into his voice. "Then we can just drive around."

"Whatever you say, man."

Twenty minutes later, when John climbed into Keith's Corvette, he was still in a great

181

mood. He immediately started pawing through Keith's CDs.

"So what's up?" John asked as he popped a Political Action Committee CD into the player. "What's with the big secrecy act?"

Keith pulled up to a stoplight and clicked on his left turn signal. He didn't have any idea where they were going—it didn't matter. "John, I'm in major trouble," he said, reaching out to turn the music down. "You've got to help me."

John shifted around in his seat so that he was facing Keith. "What kind of trouble?"

Little by little, Keith told John his story: meeting Tony at Mr. Martin's, discovering Pinewoods and seeing Tony there, losing everything, getting a loan from Tony, losing again, the phone call, the threat.

When Keith finished, John was very quiet. Keith glanced at him and guessed that he was turning all of this information over in his head. "You're in really deep, man," John finally said.

"You think I don't know that?" Keith asked sharply.

"You said you wanted my help," John said. "You've got to know I don't have that kind of cash."

"I'm not asking for a loan."

"Then what are you asking?"

Keith kept his eyes on the road. "This guy Tony wants me to throw the opening game." John didn't comment, so Keith rushed on. "I can't do it by myself. You're the quarterback. You could do it."

"Man, you're insane!" John exploded. "No way would I cheat! Besides, Walnut Hills is one of the worst teams in the league. That game's as good as ours."

"Right," Keith said desperately. "We're the favorite by a mile. And Tony knows plenty of people who'll put money on us. Enough to pay off what I owe him and then some, if we lose."

"You're pathetic," John said with disgust.

"I'm asking you as a friend," Keith pleaded.

"A friend wouldn't ask that. I won't do it."

Pulling up to another light, Keith glanced at John. His jaw was set, his arms were crossed in front of his chest, and he was staring out the window. Keith's anger flared. How dare John Badillo get all high and mighty on him? John might look like the perfect picture of wounded innocence, but Keith knew what lay underneath.

The light turned green. Keith punched the gas pedal. "I think you'd better reconsider," he said coldly as the Corvette shot forward.

"Why?"

"Because of Katia. I know you're in love with my sister."

"So?" John's voice was cold. "You think Katia would want me to lose on purpose? You know, it's illegal, what you want me to do."

"Maybe it is," Keith said. "But if you really love my sister, you'll do it."

"That sounds like a threat."

Keith shrugged casually. "Let's just say I heard that you and Victoria were all over each other in my sister's hospital room—while she was fighting for her life. She's never going to believe you love her if I tell her that."

Keith waited for John to deny it, but he didn't say a word. Keith smiled grimly as the silence continued. Up until that moment, he hadn't been sure it was true. Now Keith knew he had John right where he wanted him.

About the Author

Jennifer Baker is the author of two dozen young adult and middle grade novels. She is also the producer for TV Guide Online's teen area and teaches creative writing workshops for elementary and junior high school students. She lives in New York City with her husband and son.

Summer

by
Katherine Applegate

Three Months. Three Guys.
One Incredible Summer.

June Dreams
51030-4/$3.50

July's Promise
51031-2/$3.50

August Magic
51032-0/$3.50

Simon & Schuster Mail Order
200 Old Tappan Rd., Old Tappan, N.J. 07675
Please send me the audio I have checked above. I am enclosing $_____(please add $3.95 to cover postage and handling plus your applicable local sales tax). Send check or money order — no cash or C.O.D.'s please. Allow up to six weeks for delivery. You may use VISA/MASTERCARD: card number, expiration date and customer signature must be included.
Name _____

Address _____

City _____ State/Zip _____

VISA/MASTERCARD Card # _____ Exp.Date _____

Signature _____ 1088-02

Printed in the United States
By Bookmasters